KAFKA
GOES TO
HAVANA

KAFKA
GOES TO
HAVANA

A Novel by

Ron Savage

NEWPULP PRESS

NEW PULP PRESS

Published by New Pulp Press, LLC, 926 Truman Avenue, Key West, Florida 33040, USA.

For information contact:
Publisher@NewPulpPress.com

ISBN-13: 978-1945734182 (New Pulp Press)
ISBN-10: 1945734183

Printed in the United States of America
Visit us on the web at www.newpulppress.com

"Are you waiting for somebody?"
"For a sledge to pick me up," K. said.
"No sledges pass here," said the man. "There's no traffic here."
"But it's the road leading to the Castle," objected K.
"All the same, all the same," said the man with a certain finality, "there's no traffic here."

– Franz Kafka*
The Castle

---

* All chapter quotes are from Franz Kafka

KAFKA
GOES TO
HAVANA

HIS LEFT HAND

"I'm surprised you don't realize how insulting your suggestions are and what they imply about me, although I certainly acknowledge your good intentions."

– The Trial

Near the Old Town Square
Prague, Czech Republic

PERHAPS HER SON'S RASH on his left hand was stress related, Judita had seen a flurry of rashes this past year, year and a half. Lots of skin issues were aggravated by stress.

She'd seen it over and over again in her practice. But lately more than a few children had something going on with their skin – or so it seemed. And adults weren't that far behind their children. Skin had always announced our worries. Rashes thrived in bad times – the death of someone close, kids failing at academics, adults losing a job, etcetera, etcetera. Anything, really. Watching the TV news could do it, daily reports on endless, far away wars, children killing teachers and other children, many, many children, an economy close to world bankruptcy, the climate shifting to extremes.

Judita was surprised people weren't hurling themselves off buildings.

"When did you notice this?" she said, examining her son's fingers. They were at the green Formica kitchen table. The overhead florescent light flickered. Once in awhile it buzzed and hummed. "—Franz, sweetheart? Are you listening?"

"Uh-huh, I don't know," the boy said. "A couple of days, I think."

Judita Hoffmann was a GP who worked at the university medical school, a ten minute drive from their home. The doctor had practiced medicine for close to sixteen years. She'd a sweet face, the sort that caught the smiles of strangers. Her black hair was bobbed and done in a perm, her arms and calves a bit more fleshy than she would have liked. Judita looked up at her son. "What can I tell you, my darling? We'll monitor and see where it goes, yes?"

"What does that mean?" Franz was twelve.

"Pay attention to it," his mother said. The sides of her son's fingers were enflamed and weepy – some type of rogue atopic dermatitis. What threw off her diagnosis were tiny web-like growths in the valleys between the boy's fingers. She said, "If you see it's getting worse, you tell me."

"Am I going to die?"

"*You*?" his mother gave a little snort, something to shoo away his fear. "Oh Please. Boys like you outlive everybody."

"Is that true?"

Judita kissed his forehead. "Mostly, yes, my love," she said and quickly put a fingertip to his lips to quiet any protest. Nowadays the rules were changing too fast. A rash wasn't simply a rash, anymore. No reported deaths, thank God, not yet. But there were complications, nothing her boy needed to know. "People don't die from what you've got," she said. "There's medicine, ointments, pills, a little something for everyone. Just don't scratch."

"You promise, right?"

Judita hesitated. Knew she'd hesitated; knew he'd get anxious *because* she hesitated. It was that terrible word – *promise*. She never knew what to do with it. Parents and doctors ought not to say what they didn't know. Surely a simple rash wasn't a crisis. It wasn't a cancer or the black death. What could a person tell a patient, one's child? More than once she'd imagined her son on his death bed saying, "– But you *prom*ised."

Franz was watching her now with a look that wanted a guarantee. "Mama? You promise I'll be okay?"

"As much as any person can, honey."

Judita remembered the 7 year old girl who'd been driven to emergency by the child's father, a balding man with a puffy, damp face and thick rimless glasses, his face without expression. The girl was wrapped in a pale blue bedsheet.

"My Saskie tried to bite me," he said.

"–You're daughter?"

"Look here." The man held out his hand, his long, slender fingers trembling. "You can see the marks. Look at what my daughter did to her own father, the man who loves her more than his miserable life." The daughter had bored a tiny hole into his skin. As he talked about it, tears filled the man's eyes; spilled onto his cheeks, his chin. "Then my child tried to suck her own father's blood. I could feel the pressure on my hand."

Saskie watched her father talking.

Judita Hoffmann remembered how beautiful the child looked, her large blue eyes, the cropped white-blond hair, a few loose strands about her cheeks and forehead. The doc had removed the sheet, and the girl's body looked frail and worn. Judita wanted to scoop her up and take care of her forever.

Blood still crusted at the corners of Saskie's mouth. She'd watched her father talk and now and again she would smile to herself. What bothered Hoffman was the girl's body, no more than stretched skin over bones. That would've been bad enough, a child half starved, but a shiny, iridescent shell covered Saskie's shoulders and the curve of her back. The iridescence had a dark green tint to it. Judita thought of the June bugs she use to capture in the summer – she was Saskie's age then – and she had tied them to a string and let them fly about her head.

THINGS TO DO IN THE NIGHT

"I could write more about your influence on the wider circles of our life, and the opposing struggles, but here I am uncertain and would have to infer things ..."
— Letter to My Father

SEE IF IT'S HER, Franz thought. The woman had come to mind. He didn't know her name but he called her the Wolf Lady. She had a lot of black hair, very thick, very frizzy, and some of the hair stood up on her head like ears. Most times she wore a white T-shirt under a black leather motorcycle jacket that had silver zippers running from cuff to elbow She'd faded rolled up jeans and black boots. Once Franz had seen her sitting across the street on a park bench under a sodium lamp with her jacket off. Her arms were powdered with dark shiny hair.

"Was that you?" he whispered

Franz remembered the particular sound that had awakened him.

Tat-tat.

A sound loud enough to hear, odd enough to end his sleep. Moonlight crossed the wood floor of his bedroom. The light came from the open window. Gauzy beige curtains billowed in the cold air. The boy looked down at his bandaged left hand. His mother had rubbed the area with some type of menthol smelling cream then wrapped it in clean white gauze before he'd gone to bed.

"We all have our burdens," Judita had said earlier, and kissed his forehead.

Now his fingers were throbbing, the pain coming in and receding like the tide. It wasn't a new "condition" – what his parents called it. The hand had been bothering the boy for a few months.

The *tat-tat* noise that had awakened him twenty minutes, a half-hour ago brought the dream of a carpenter striking a nail into a piece of wood.

"Go to the window," Franz said to himself, his words lazy from sleep. He would *not* be afraid. He'd just turned twelve last month and boys his age shouldn't be getting all worked up over nothing. Maybe the person was outside. Maybe the Wolf Lady was fixing a loose board on her bench.

An investigation was needed. The idea of being a detective appealed to him. Franz wanted to overcome his fears. Fear held a person back. Fear caused people to accept second best. Fear caused regret. He believed fearful things were usually the most interesting things. And the most interesting things can change your life. The boy saw himself as a person who valued clues.

Franz thought of the close times with his father. They'd watched the old private eye movies, the black and white ones, especially the *Maltese Falcon*. The boy would tell his father he wanted to be Sam Spade when he grew up. He'd say it because he loved Spade's fedora and trench coat. The boy also believed he said it to please his dad.

A nod, a smile, anything his father gave him was deeply felt.

"Can you picture me in a fedora, papa?"

No answer.

"Do they make those coats for children?"

Nothing.

6

Franz's legs left the warmth of the wool blanket. The boy sat on the edge of the bed and looked about the room. He wore white shorts and a gray T-shirt. Franz was holding his hand wrapped in gauze close to his chest. He couldn't stop the throbbing in his stupid fingers and thumb.

He remembered Karl watching the roll and flicker of the old movie on their living room TV. His dad was small and muscular with dark eyes and thick dark hair. Franz had the same dark eyes and hair, but the boy was more brain than muscle, what his father had told him, a boy too skinny for serious fighting.

"You remind me of my brother," his father said. "You're clones, you and Max. It's uncanny. I was the oldest but I always looked up to my brother, probably more than he ever looked up to me."

Karl taught biology at the university; specifically, he studied bugs. His father told him that a person who studies bugs is called an entomologist. He'd said, "What I do is look at the genetic regulatory proteins of bugs and the DNA sequences of these proteins."

"I don't know what that means." his son said.

"I study why bugs do what they do." Karl said, "Your Uncle Max does the same type of work but in another country."

"Why doesn't he just work with you?" Franz didn't get it.

"Prague wasn't big enough for the two of us," his father said, half joking, half not. Karl had many interests. He liked telling his son, "I'm more well-rounded person than your uncle."

The boy guessed that was true. His father painted. That year his watercolors appeared in two of the local galleries. In one gallery he'd entered his paintings in a contest and won a smoked ham. Karl enjoyed literature, too. His favorite author was Franz Kafka whose childhood home was less than a kilometer away near the *Staroměstské náměstí*, the old town square.

"I have felt just as bewildered as brother Kafka, just as alienated from my life," his father liked to say. "He is my true kinsman. Both of us have battled tedious lives. Both of us have had our imaginations terrify us." Once Karl taught a seminar on the writer at their local library.

The father had also named his son Franz, after the author.

Franz recalled watching the *Maltese Falcon* with his dad and saying, "I wish Sam Spade was real so he'd teach me to become a detective." The boy had often confused Sam Spade and Franz Kafka, as if his father's favorites were one person – one exploring the outside, one exploring the inside. "Being a detective is the best job. How amazing to have such a job, poppa."

That TV night Franz had hoped for a smile, a shrug, something.

"Did you and Uncle Max want to be detectives when you were my age?"

"All boys want to be detectives."

Tat-tat. That was the sound, exactly. *Tat-tat*.

Franz walked over to the half-open bedroom window. The cold night air rushed about his face, his bare arms. The wood bench across the street was empty. Lamplight circled the bench in a yellow glow. See, it's nothing, he thought. A dream. Case solved, case closed. But the boy couldn't quit thinking about it. He stared at the window, frost collecting at the edges of the glass panes.

The Wolf Lady liked sitting there. He'd seen her on the park bench at least three time this week. Franz was sure she had followed his father to work.

"Don't be silly," Karl Hoffmann had said. "Do I look like a movie star to you? Am I a rich man in a fine, rich suit?"

The boy had also seen the Wolf Lady following him and his mother to his school.

"She's a person just like you and me," his mother told him. "She has a condition, too. You of all people should understand a condition. It's called *hirsutism*, that's when people have more hair than they know what to do with." Then Judita said, "Honestly, darling, you must try having more compassion."

The boy wasn't sure how long the Wolf Lady had been watching their house and following them. Maybe three months, he didn't know, precisely.

Tat-tat.

You will *not* be afraid, Franz thought; a bit of a reprimand. You're almost an adult, act like it. Mother said she has *hirsutism*, it's just hair. How can you be afraid of hair? Maybe one of his parents had walked past the door. It could be as simple as that. The family bathroom was at the end of the hall. Surely the noise had come from one of his parents, probably his father. His father peed all night.

"You worry about everything," mother liked to remind him. She was a woman with a thick waist and curled reddish-brown hair. Her clothes were bright; flower prints, mostly. She'd tease him and say, "Tell me, Franz, did the devil take your smile?" Sometimes Franz thought of himself as an adopted child but an adopted child who lived in a comfortable home with parents who adored him. This mysterious feeling left him sad.

The bedroom floor was cool under his feet. Franz leaned his ear to the door.

"Hello?" he said, louder this time. The noise that woke him had come and gone. He opened the door enough to peek down the shadowed hallway and look at his parents' closed bedroom door. That's when he imagined his mother calling him.

"Franz, I need you," her voice weak, frightened. How many times had he heard her that way? And what if it were true? he thought. What if she *did* need me? How would I act? What would I do? "...help us, Franz."

The boy began running the carpeted hallway toward his parents' bedroom. He didn't care if his mother's voice was imaginary or not. What was more important than his mother needing him?

"...Mama," Franz murmured, all breathy.

The boy ran through the darkness and the lamplight. He paused at his parents' door. A vague yellow glow seeped into the hallway from the bedroom.

Franz paused, took a deep breath and let it go. Then he walked into the room. That's when he pressed his lips firmly together to stop a scream.

His mother and father sat with their backs pressed against the mahogany headboard. They had open books on their laps but they were looking at him, or looking straight ahead.

That was it, he thought. They were looking straight ahead at nothing. His mother wore her pink nightgown, baby roses with a green leaf print. His father had on a sleeveless undershirt, what he wore regardless of the weather. At the center of each of their foreheads was a dark red circle the size of a dime.

Tat-tat.

Franz backed himself into a shadowy corner, feeling his legs giving way. He crumbled onto the wood floor, the cold, hard boards, pieces of him slipping away in separate directions.

The boy tried understanding what he saw but couldn't look at his mother and father long enough to figure it out. The gauze about his hand had become loose and it fell away. His index and middle fingers were fused together, bone and flesh. Bristled hair sprouted on what had been his knuckles and backhand. The fingers were shaped like a claw.

HIS BROTHER'S SON

"...he really wanted to transform his room into a cave...it would have let him forget his past when he had still been human."

— Metamorphosis

Oración a la Milagrosa Polyclinic
Havana, Cuba

THE TWO OF them were seated in her office, surrounded by morning sunlight.

"You're not married?" the psychologist wanted to know.

"I never felt the need."

"And this nephew, you have no relationship with him?"

"I'm here. He's in Prague." The man spoke English in a Czech accent.

Dr. Coro Acosta could hear the nuances in the man's voice, his anxiety. He didn't like the situation. But the secrets people kept were often more common than unique. Some find this revelation depressing. She knew one thing for certain. He wanted her to play mother to his soon arriving nephew, or at least the child's therapist. Fine, no surprise. Most people would see a twelve year old with dead parents and no place to go as a problem to avoid.

He looked terrified.

"I can imagine your concerns," Acosta said. "Many people would flee from your task. A bachelor, a man who values solitude, especially that sort of person. Devotion to the intellect isn't a family sport, is it? I'm surprised you haven't fled the country."

"It's crossed my mind."

Maximilian Hoffmann actually smiled, brief and gone, but an actual smile. He was small and eerily white, a full step beyond pale. A man who...what? Liked staying in the darkness? Yes, that was it, exactly.

A regular dose of Cuban sunshine could've solved the problem. He must prefer darkness, she thought – and all the fantasies that the darkness implied. Secrecy, protection, comfort for a few uneasy souls, or that was what came to her mind. Dr. Acosta wondered if sunlight had ever touched the poor fellow. His skin was translucent, too, showing complex paths of veins. She could see a heartbeat at the sides of his neck. More that that, he looked hungry. She imagined his skin flushed and ordinary after a good meal, the pulse less noticeable; a better disposition, maybe.

Professor Hoffmann's black hair and eyes just add to his unique appearance – ah, the perfect word ... *unique*, a non-offensive word but one indicating the way he caught the eye, stirred uncomfortable feelings, revealed a gloomier fantasy. She felt concern for the nephew's safety.

The child just left one tragedy, he didn't need another.

This is nobody's father, Coro thought.

Shadow and light played on the concrete floor and the dingy navy blue tile walls of Dr. Acosta's office. The wood door frame was chocolate brown and sections of it were flaking and scratched. Patient and doctor sat across from one another in beige plastic chairs. Acosta still couldn't shake off the embarrassment of her office, the dirt on the walls, the uneven concrete floor, the smell of fish and banana frying in the restaurant next door. The psychologist had been raised by Cuban American parents in Springfield, Massachusetts. She and her mother had returned to Havana several years ago. Coro felt ashamed about being embarrassed. After all there was poverty in Massachusetts, too. Cuba didn't have an exclusivity on poor people. But the poverty in American was different than the poverty in Cuba. Everybody who was poor in Cuba was Cuban.

"Will you or won't you see my nephew?" Professor Hoffmann said. Acosta heard his impatience. Then the professor said, "Look, I mean no disrespect." He took a breath to calm himself. "I cannot tell you what a shock it was to hear of my brother's passing. The mother, too. What a generous person. I can only guess at the boy's sorrow."

"Franz's sorrow."

"What?"

"That's your nephew's name, isn't it? Franz."

"I don't understand?"

"You called him 'the boy,' I believe." She'd tried for a friendly tone but it sounded too sarcastic, maybe too accusatory. "I'm sure I see too much in that."

"No, no. You're right, of course. He isn't 'the boy.' He's my brother's child. He's got a name. Yes, of course. The boy – I mean, Franz – will take getting used to."

This was a good sign, she thought. A man who can self-reflect is a man who isn't afraid to see himself as less than perfect – any man *or* woman – that was the whole therapeutic battle, the talent to self-reflect. If a person could do that, a person could do therapy. To accurately and impartially see one's part, Dr. Acosta thought her job could be reduced to those few words. *Toaccurately and impartially see one's part*. That's why depressed patients do so much better than paranoid patients. The depressed feel responsible for whatever comes their way while the paranoid seek a solution in others. With the depressed patient, you'll find yourself saying, "Well, yes, you did do such and such, but you didn't do *all* of it." With the paranoid patient, the opposite is true. The therapist will says, "Well, yes, they did do such and such, but they didn't do *all* of it."

And adding, "What was your part in the event?" It seldom varied.

"I'm one of two child psychologists in Havana," Coro Acosta is saying to Professor Hoffmann. "Three million people and there are only two of us." Coro was in her thirties, thin and dark complected, her hair corn-rolled in tight braids, her large eyes dark as her skin. She said, "I can't begin to tell you how valuable my time is, professor."

"Does this mean no?"

"I think it means I want assurances."

"I don't understand." His irritation had returned. With it, a weariness.

Dr. Acosta looked at him, this strangely put together man. She tried picturing him doing fatherly things. Nothing came to her mind – no pictures of ballgames or teaching the child the family trade or giving him lessons in self-defense. She said, "Tell me the truth. Do you want to raise this child? Even under the best circumstances, raising a child is daunting. It's not what a parent does some of the time, not parents who're good at it."

"What choice do I have?" Max said, resignation in his tone. "You can expect a sense of duty, of obligation," he said. "That I can give you, promise you. My brother is – *was* – a decent man. I don't forget such things. I was the youngest, but I protected him. I know how to do that, protect the person I love. I often believed Karl was a young soul, impulsive, given to drama in situations that were less than ordinary. Maybe love will come, doctor, maybe it won't. Who among us can predict the future?"

He was right. What could she expect? Coro Acosta was listening to the professor as she wrote her notes. She often wrote notes in a therapy session, or an interview. She couldn't be expected to remember all the thoughts that crossed her mind. Who knew what would be important or not, the exact link that could tie one statement to another. She'd often thought of using a video camera, but she couldn't afford such luxuries. How wonderful, though, watching her patient and herself interacting, to spot what she could've done differently, could've done better, how instructive to see all the subtleties that had escaped her.

"I don't speak German," Acosta said, reading over what she'd written. The man had quit speaking a couple of minutes ago. Maybe more, maybe less, she wasn't sure."–Or Czech. I speak Spanish and English. Does the boy speak English?"

No answer.

Coro glanced up and looked about the office. How gritty and worn everything looked in the morning. The tile walls, the glass in the windows, the chocolate painted door, sunlight had its own cruelties. Professor Hoffmann was gone – not a sound, no footfall against the concrete floor, no open and closing the door, no By Your Leave. Who walks out of an office without a good-bye? These were the manners of a child. He lacked basic interpersonal skills. Or he had the skills but didn't think she was worth the effort.

THE CLOJET

THE BOY HAD taken Transavia at Vaclav Havel Airport to Paris, then Air France at Orly to Havana. The attendants gave him food and soda and praised him for being a child that didn't cause a fuss. But not everyone thought that. He'd slept a bit on both planes and one of his dreams had caused the older French woman beside him to shake his shoulder. Then the woman put an index finger to her lips and said, "The young gentleman must keep his dreams to himself." She spoke to him in English but with a heavy French accent. Why English, he didn't know. Her fleshy underarms quivered when she folded them, a little motion of finality. The attendant had overheard the woman and whispered to her, told her Franz found his parents m.u.r.d.e.r.e.d. Yes, spelled it. Like the boy was a refugee who couldn't spell.

"Everyone has problems," the woman said to the attendant. "Everyone suffers. You think I don't suffer?"

Franz was remembering his dream very well. The dream was about what had happened the night he had gone into his parents' bedroom. He'd been sitting in a dark corner of his parents' room, arms about his legs, knees pressed to his chest. Everything inside him was twitching. He waited for his mother and father to notice him. Their eyes were open, but neither of them had moved. Dolls, that's what he thought. They weren't his real parents. They were dolls that *looked* like his parents. A tiny red circle dotted each forehead. Like they'd suddenly become Hindus, what some go through to deny bullet holes. Then he couldn't get it out of his mind. They'd been shot. That was a bullet hole, Franz reappraising the situation. He could even see the blood on the headboard in back of them. Bits of stuff, too, brain and skull probably.

No, no. No, no.

He felt the cold night coming through the open bedroom window. Where the killer had entered, the boy figured. The Wolf Lady? Finally. At last. He imagined her no longer denying her animal thirst. He preferred looking at the window than seeing the red spattered wall behind his parents.

Okay, maybe all the blood and the bits of stuff wasn't on the wall. Darkness could have caused his eyes to trick him. That sort of thing happened all the time. The light, the shadow – who knew every game the night played? Franz wanted his father to ragefully order him out of the bedroom; wanted the old man to get flush faced. He wanted to see the veins get puffy on his neck and forehead. Franz wanted his mother to pat his father's arm and go *shhh, shhh*, and calm the man.

Come on you two, he thought.

"Perhaps our baby boy had a bad dream, dear," that's what he'd like his mom to say, a voice of reason in an unreasonable world. She'd say, "Children always want their parents when they have bad dreams."

"Mama's right," Franz said; to himself, mostly. He looked at his father, "I had a terrible dream, poppa. Please don't get quiet on me. *Please*. Boys can have terrible dreams. Boys can ask for things. There's no law against that. Boys and girls aren't that different, poppa. We get scared, too – girls *and* boys."

"See, dear," his mother nudging his father. "Tell the boy we're dead." Franz imagined his father saying this as though being dead were no different than going to the bakery for rolls and a pastry.

"That's *not* what mothers do," Franz's mother said. "We help and praise. We make a safe world for our babies."

His parents were still sitting in the bed, their books open and facing down on their laps. The reading lamps on the two nightstands made dim yellow spotlights in the darkness.

Father's bullet hole was seeping blood. The blood had rolled over his left eyebrow and down the left side of his nose. A drop paused on the upper lip, teetered at the edge before falling onto the chest of his sleeveless undershirt. The splotch of red nestled in the white cloth.

Franz turned away; looked for a different scene again, something that would take him from the blood and his parents' useless eyes.

This is when he saw the half opened closet door. That did *not* happen in his father's bedroom. Karl Hoffmann was a man who locked things down. He had the same routine night after night – lock the bedroom door, shut the closet door, put his slippers next to his side of the bed just so. A place for everything and everything in its place, that was Karl Hoffmann.

"I'll close the closet door," Franz said.

He waited for his father to say, "–None of your business boy. Go back to your room."

Nothing.

"Okay then," Franz said. The boy would rather have had his father yelling at him than to deal with his silence. Franz stood and brushed whatever dirt clung to the bottom of his jockeys. "Here I go now. Going to close the door. You stop me if you want," he said in the direction of his father's expressionless face but not specifically looking at him. "I know it's not my business. This is *your* room, poppa. I know that. Believe me, I have never been the foolish boy you think I am ... *thought* I was."

Franz tried to stop obsessing about that horrific night, shook himself from it – his parents propped up in the bed, their eyes all wrong, the fear that covered him like hot breath – released himself from the terror.

The older woman on the plane next to Franz was asleep, her head tilted toward him, her mouth partially open. Her lipstick had worn itself into stale pink, the color caught in the tiny creases of her upper lip. Bits of white saliva pooled at the corners of her mouth.

He imagined her waggling a finger at him; saying, "Mothers and fathers die every day. The young gentleman should understand this as soon as possible. Nobody cares about you, or your pathetic life. You're *not* special. You don't *own* tragedy. Am I being clear, you spoiled, insignificant insect? The world doesn't revolve around you and your creepy, so-dead parents.

Children! Thank God I never indulged myself. Could children be any more tedious? I think not – in fact, I *know* it."

Some of that he made up.

Franz shut his eyes again. He was trapped – the plane or his parents' bedroom. The same nightmare followed him. He preferred his parents, their awful deaths. I'm not an insignificant insect, he thought. I am the son of my parents, they know me, they loved me, or my mother loved me. I know *she* loved me, I know that much. Okay, his father, too – his father loved him, Franz was almost sure.

How many times had his dad told him, "You have a good mind, boy. I know a good mind and you've got one. Use the brain God gave you. I can't be here all the time, holding your hand, telling you what to do. You *must* learn to trust your thinking. Become a confident person, a person with critical reasoning. Without critical reasoning, we're nothing but animals looking for dinner."

Fine, all right. Franz remembered being in his dead parents' bedroom and gazing into their shadowed closet.

He expected to see his mother and father's shoes in neat, straight rows. Their clothes would be draped on wood hangers; mother's clothes to the left, father's clothes to the right. He expected a fastidiousness to every dress, blouse, pair of pants and starched shirt.

He got none of that.

Shoes were scattered, intermingled, a man's polished black dress shoe realigned with a woman's scuffed brown pump. Clothes had been pulled from their hangers. Pants and blouses were strewn across the dark floor.

The killer had done this, Franz thought. He pictured Sam Spade putting two and two together, ready to spot the clues. What would Sam do? the boy's question of the night. A case like this required observations.

"Critical reasoning," the imagined voice of his dead father corrected him.

Franz thought, No time to feel sorry for myself – no being afraid or sad or crying.

He heard his dead father again, "This job isn't for whiny baby boys.

Franz had to stay tough. This case took a boy who could put his feelings aside. No tears tonight, no Oh What Will I Do Now, none of that embarrassing childish business.

"People want a professional," his dead father scolded.

"I'm *very* professional," Franz whispered, feeling insulted. Why would his father say such a hurtful thing?

"Good, excellent. I knew I could count on you."

"You won't be ashamed, father."

Probably the Wolf Lady had found the sliding wall panel to the rear of the closet. Who else had the slyness, the animal-keen perception, the intuition guided one to the right choice?

"So you're blaming the poor woman with *hirsutism*?" his dead mother said. "Who are you to make these judgments? Where is your proof? How have I failed you?"

Who needed proof? he thought. This was a detective's hunch.

The real question, the *true* question was this: had this person known about the panel and the hidden room behind it, *or* was the room revealed by poking here and there? Hired assassin types don't stumble upon these sort of doors, Franz believed, especially the Wolf Lady. You don't put a bullet into the heads of a boy's parents on a whim and not know about the victim's secret room.

"There you go," his dead father said. "Critical thinking."

The wood panel still embedded in the side of the wall, the narrow opening a thicker darkness in an already dark place. The secret panel and the secret room were his father's inventions, a hideout Sydney Greenstreet and Peter Lori might have built. But did the killer find what he or she had wanted? Who could see in here without a flashlight or knew the whereabouts of the light switch?

An investigation was needed, Franz thought, definitely in Sam Spade mode now. The boy was no stranger to this room. His father had "almost" naked pictures of women in his bottom desk drawer, an old fashion roll top desk. The women were overweight and dressed in bathing suits that looked like shorts and a sort of shapeless top. These were antique photos, belonging to Franz's grandfather, maybe great-grandfather. Along with the photos was an old stereopticon viewer. He'd discovered this hideaway one rainy Saturday afternoon, his dad still at work, his mother downstairs preparing a chicken stew and biscuits. The room was small and the light came from a green shaded banker's lamp on the desk.

Franz never told anyone.

The boy didn't want his father to lock him out of the hideout, or whatever it was. He had found something else there minutes after he'd found the pictures of the chubby women in shorts. A small tan leather book was hidden under a false bottom of the drawer on the top left side. His father's diary, or something like a diary, it's pages written in black ink, a neat, small cursive. The book had to do with many things, his father's work at the university, descriptions about everyday events, whatever struck him. That night Franz had sat at the roll top desk. He looked under the false bottom of the drawer on the top left side. The Wolf Lady hadn't been clever enough to find the diary.

AT HOME WITH THE WOLF LADY

*"Instead of feeling his way with the prudence befitting
the greatness of his enemy and of his ambition, he had
spent a whole night wallowing in puddles of beer."*
— The Castle

San Francisco de Paula
70 km. Outside Havana

ENTOMOLOGY ISN'T FOR those troubled by
diversity. Lottie liked telling this to her wife, Aria, the
Egyptian. That conversation started years ago —
twenty, twenty-five years. Aria was a tolerant person in
many ways —political views, infirmities, religious
affiliations, sexual preferences. But first, and most
important, she did not mind Lottie's hair.

"Egyptian men and women are very hairy," she'd
say. "Not all, of course, but many. It's, you know, quite
sexy, having all that hair. Like making love to an animal
— a bear, a sheep, what-have-you. And what's wrong
with that? Nothing."

Right now Lottie's thick black hair was pulled back
and secured with rubber bands and two silver
barrettes, her frizzed, wild look subdued but not tamed.
She had on a white T-shirt and beige, thigh length
shorts that showed the hair on her thin arms and legs.
None of it had ever struck Aria as outrageous. Present,
yes; soft, yes. Oddly sensual, oh you bet. But the woman

25

wasn't looking at you through a haystack of hair.

"This is what I adore about you." Lottie said, a gentle voice. "You curl up next to me like I'm your fur coat." Then she hesitated, a beat or two, before saying, "Yet you don't care for my collection. You tolerate it, you do that. But no real interest, yes?"

"If I'd known you were a bug collector, I would've made another life choice," Aria partly kidding and partly not. "Become a nun. *Some*thing, I dunno."

She took another sip of her red. Aria and Lottie had been sitting on the front porch and drinking for most of the afternoon. Lottie had just brought out smoked cheese and herb bread, all local. She placed the tan wood bread and cheese tray on a small round wicker table.

"And now?" Lottie grinned, knowing the answer.

"Well now I'm hooked, you more than the bugs."

"You better say that."

Insects in display cases hung on the white walls of their home. Each specimen had its Latin name beneath its pinned body. Teakwood tables in the living room and the study held additional display cases.

"I still don't like bugs in our home," Aria said.

"When I think about it, I can see how envious I am," Lottie said. "My step-brothers are these big deal professors – entomologists. Even when they were kids, they both liked insects. I guess I wanted them to stop making fun of me – Karl more than Max. But I also wanted them to know I was smart, too."

Both Aria and Lottie were well into their forties. Aria could already see gray threading her hair. For each strand she would pluck, two took its place. Growing old wasn't for the timid. Old*er*, Aria thought. *Not* old. She even had the beginning of a tummy. A tummy, for god-sake.

"It's been me and you forever, hasn't it?" Aria said.

"I wouldn't have it any other way."

Aria smiled and lit a cigarette. The smile didn't last very long. She looked at the painted buildings along San Francisco de Paula's narrow main street, a few were blue, three bright green, and the owner of the local cafe had recently painted his place mauve. Aria's and Lottie's house was adobe natural, drab when compared to the others.

"Are you going to tell me about your trip?" Aria said. She exhaled smoke and waved it away from Lottie, simultaneously. "I mean you go off in the middle of the night. I don't see you for a week – no call, no nothing."

"It was Prague. And I left at 6:30 in the evening."

"C'mon. Who goes to *Prague*?"

"I was born there," Lottie said. "Abused there, too. I told you all that, you know my secrets – what my older brother, Karl, did to me? How he burned the hair off my arms and legs? The other one, the younger brother, Max, he left me alone. He was a more to himself person. But Karl was just evil. He once found me in the bed with the girl from the house next to us. She and I, we were ten, I think. Karl beat me so hard I couldn't close my right eye for a week. He was only two years older but shit he could hit, you know? At first I used to blame myself – for being *dif*ferent. But Karl was just an asshole." Lottie smiled to herself, then a quick shrug. "Nothing like going through the old scrapbook."

"So a family reunion?"

"Yeah, cake and ice cream."

Aria knew Lottie was adopted by a Prague couple before her first birthday. Mama Hoffmann had found her in the alley across the street from their home. The infant was covered with a wet gray wool blanket and laid next to a garbage can. Baby Lottie was half frozen and covered in her own shit, doomed from the get-go.

"Did you visit your Karl and his wife?" Aria said,

studying her wine glass, pushing for hints. "Is that it? Don't they have a little boy?"

"He's twelve. But, yeah, little for twelve."

"See, I'm guessing you've gone back to the life," Aria said, for the umpteenth time in their relationship. "I'm not going to lie. I think you just couldn't stay away, what I'm guessing. It's like having another lover you can't shake. And, of course, I start feeling like the poor fucked up victim."

"Let's not play the drama queen."

"Please, allow me a moment." Aria sliced a thin bit of cheese and laid it on a piece of herb bread. She was looking at a fat boy chasing a rooster in an erratic, dusty circle on the main road. The boy stopped and rested his palms on his brown pudgy knees, sucking in a couple of deep breaths. Aria watched the boy as she talked, "I start thinking how our everyday life is too mundane for the adrenaline junky Lottie Hoffmann."

"That's not true. You know that's not true."

"But you did go somewhere and murder someone. Don't say you didn't; please don't tell me how crazy I am, or how immature and clingy I am." Aria poured herself more red from the glass carafe. "Who in Prague has gone to their reward? *Whom*, I mean. Hopefully it's not bubba and the wife. I dunno, I *should* be more outraged at what you do – your, whatever, *vocation*. Which says something about me, doesn't it? My lack of moral conscience, my need for collusion."

Lottie put an index finger to her lips, glanced to see if anyone was nearby. "Are you nuts?" she whispered, almost a hiss. "How long have you and I been together? What's the number one rule?"

"Never talk about Fight Club?"

"You think this is a joke?" Lottie was giving her The Look. If a look could kill, Aria thought. Lottie hadn't left whisper mode, "You think this is funny? Is that it?

Why don't you discuss this with the fat boy and the rooster. You want our lives ruined? You want me in jail? You want our home taken away?"

"You should ask yourself those questions."

"How do you think we afford this place? You're like some college girl who eats burgers and talks about how *ethically* wrong it is to slaughter cows." Lottie stopped and took a breath. "I'm going to quit talking now and we're never discussing this again."

Aria took Lottie's hand. Lottie tried pulling away but Aria held on tight and said, "You don't think I'm on your side? You worry the shit out of me. I know what you do, I'm no fool."

The two became quiet, both staring in opposite directions, a minute, less, more – time had shed its clues. Aria said, "...so what *did* you do, kill Karl and his wife?"

THE
INVESTIGATION

"...but your character was so different from ours," she said, "that, even when you spoke frankly, it was bound to be difficult for us to believe you."

– The Castle

Near the Old Town Square Hotel
Prague

INSPECTOR DOMINIK KOPECKY hated this area of town, the *Staroměstské náměstí*.

Oh it was lovely, the enormous town square with its shops and cafes, it's ancient bricks set like cobblestone. Many apartments and homes surrounded the square, three and four story buildings, beige, gray or slate, most with ricotta roofs. The Vltava River lingered about the periphery of Prague, the water a deep, no nonsense blue, it's bridges gothic, medieval. The city was a European jewel and it had been that for over a thousand years.

Kopecky didn't give a shit.

What bothered the inspector was the tediousness of local criminals. 61% of all crime in Prague was corruption and bribery. Bookkeepers and politicians looted each other like it was a game of Dungeons and Dragons. And, yes, there *were* other annoyances. Fucking tourists kept stealing pieces of the city, documents, chunks of statues and buildings, bricks

31

from the old town square. What the hell does a person want with a brick? A week ago Kopecky caught a team of six men from Seattle trying to dismantle a bridge at 3:20 in the morning. The Seattle Six was what a Prague newspapers called them. Our reporters *love* American journalism, Dominikthought. The *New York Post, the New York Daily News* – the Prague newspapers were all over

the Seattle Six. *Bridge Over Trouble Waters,* read one headline. *A Bridge Too Far*, read the other. Where would tabloids be without movies and songs?

Dominick Kopecky saw himself as a "squatty" man, a word he used to describe himself when he stood naked in front of the bathroom mirror. He definitely needed to lose five pounds. Okay, maybe fifteen. Okay, on a less than perfect day, conceivably twenty. He wore nice suits, though – everyone said that – with starched white shirts and elaborate, eye-catching silk ties. He had his little style going on.

Last month somebody finally murdered somebody. Inspector Kopecky was excited about it and felt ashamed he felt excited. Cases like this happened more on TV shows than real life – months could go by, a year. The homicide – a *double* homicide – occurred a block away from the *Staroměstské náměstí*.

"Are you in love?" A female colleague had asked.

She'd said that this morning when Kopecky sat at his desk, grinning to himself. He'd waved a small plastic bag in her direction. Though the bag appeared empty, it held two long, black hairs from the Hoffmann case, the double murder that had captured the inspector's time and passion. Kopecky hadn't found any prints but he did find the hairs; found them in a weird secretive area in the back of the Hoffmann's bedroom closet. The area would've been difficult to just stumble upon. More than likely the person who'd killed the Hoffmann's also knew them.

"You've got a glow," she said.

"So it must be love?"

"Usually, yes."

"A man can love many things, Ms. Nemec."

Kamila Nemec liked flirting with Dominick. She worked in records but enjoyed hearing him talk about his cases. Maybe enjoyed me for me, Kopecky thought. Kamila must have been in her early thirties; at least 15 years younger than the Inspector, not what you'd call a May-December thing, more like May-mid-August. She had short dark hair and big dark eyes. Serious ass, too; amazing ass, actually. Inspector Kopecky imagined making love to Ms. Nemec with her on top so he could grip her 10-out-of-10 ass with both hands, just digging his lucky fingers into those babies. His Nemec ass fantasy was almost as good as the Hoffmann double murder.

"I have a tanning machine" he said.

Kamila looked confused. "... a what?"

"Your question about my glow." Kopecky pointed to his face. "I bought the tanning machine to help with my seasonal depression. I mean I'm not clinically depressed, okay?" Dominick made air quotes around the words "clinically depressed." Why did he get into this? "But, you know, waiting around to do my job can be depressing. At times. The tanning machine helps that. I read it in one of those online magazines. Sunlight increases your vitamin D, and there's a relationship between low levels of vitamin D and depression." Kopecky hoped that might impress her.

"What's in your plastic baggie?" she said.

"Two hairs."

Her nose scrunched up. "This is why you're happy – two hairs?"

Kopecky felt he'd let her down. He often felt that

way when Ms. Nemec seemed bored with him. "Not *any* two hairs, Kamila. We're talking a would-be murderer."

"Well I'm sure you know what you're doing." Kamila Nemec had already gone back to separating a large stack of manila folders on her desk.

The Inspector could have told Ms. Nemec that he already had a suspect. He'd questioned the neighborhood about who'd been seen on the night of the murder, people on the street, out of the ordinary people. The coroner had put the deaths at about two or three in the morning. Most of the neighborhood was asleep and saw nothing. But 3 of the 14 people interviewed that day said they saw a woman sitting on a park bench across the street from the Hoffmann's home. "Lottie Hoffmann," an older woman had told Kopecky.

"...who?" His interest had definitely perked up.

"The step-sister." The older witness was stooped about the shoulders; late sixties, the inspector guessed. She'd said, "I hadn't seen her in years But there was no way I could have missed her. "It's the hair, you know. Once you see all that hair, you don't forget."

THE FIRST SESSION

"Almost everything you've said so far has been things we could've taken from your behavior, even if you'd said no more than a few words. And what you have said has not exactly been in your favor."

– The Trial

Oración a la Milagrosa Polyclinic
Havana, Cuba

FRANZ COULDN'T TAKE a regular breath – the best he could do were quick half breaths – and his heart kept hitting the inside of his chest. He hated the stupid clinic and he hated the doctor's tiny office with its dirty blue tile walls and its concrete floor that slanted everything. How do people live like this?

"Can you hear me?" Dr. Acosta said.

Franz nodded, his head bowed slightly, his eyes dark and wide. The boy felt sweat go down the left side of his face. He and the psychologist sat across from each other on plastic chairs. She'd just given him a paper bag.

"You're having a panic attack, okay?" Coro Acosta said. "Listen to me, pal. Cover your nose and mouth with the bag and breath in slowly. Okay? Can you do that for me? Just listen to my voice. People have panic attacks all the time. I've had one or two myself, so I know what works. The paper bag *always* works, trust me. You need a little CO2."

Franz nodded again. The brown bag started to collapse and expand with his breathing. After two or three minutes, he felt his heart return to a softer beat. Dr. Acosta was right, the bag worked.

The boy remembered the diary he'd taken from his father's secret room and he patted the right pocket of his khaki's to see if it was still there.

"What's that?" Dr. Acosta pointed to his pocket.

"Just a book," the boy said. He inhaled into the paper bag again. Father was right, nothing's private in Cuba. If people want to see your underwear, you have to pull down your pants. Everything belonged to everybody in Cuba, that's what his father had said. But Prague was like that, too – a little, anyway.

Franz hated this place.

The clinic was a nightmare – crying babies, old people curled and rocking, whispering to themselves – eighty-two clinics for three million people, what his Uncle Max had told him this morning before dropping him off to see Dr. Acosta. There were men and women with bruised faces and busted limbs here. Some were still arguing. "Baseball was the second biggest sport in Cuba," Max had said. "First prize goes to the folks who beat each other up." Franz couldn't imagine that being true.

"You doing okay, pal?" The psychologist looked up from the spiral notebook balanced on her knee and smiled at the boy. Franz saw her notice his bandaged hand. Her smile disappeared. "What happened?" Tell me about your hand."

Franz was glancing about the small office, and didn't answer. The boy imagined Dr. Coro Acosta wading through the battered and the bloody every morning, hearing their anger, their blame – a few trying to protect their already messy wounds. One or two fights would reignite and bring screams, fists searching for an opening, patients ready to finish their disputes. The ones who grabbed center stage were treated first, the violent ones, the ones who stirred the staff's anxiety. That's what Uncle Max said, what his uncle had seen on his visit here. The biggest cries, the crazies who taunted you the most, or the ones who had no control, these patients were hurried along – number uno on the staff's panic list.

What chance did a quiet boy have to get noticed? His voice wasn't the loudest, his pain could not be seen, heard or x-rayed.

"Next time, you won't have to wait," Coro Acosta said. "Just knock on the door. I made you my first appointment."

"I'm not used to crowds."

"I saw you out there," the doctor said.

The boy had seen her, too. He'd had his hands cupped over both ears to stop the noise. "Everybody's so loud," Franz said.

"Poor people are afraid of being forgotten."

Cuba was no different than any place else. Max Hoffmann had given him a lecture this morning as they drove to the clinic.

"The ones who have a dime complained about the ones who have a nickel," he'd said. "Socialism is a step up for some and a step down for others. It turns out, people who have things don't like to share with people who don't have things. Who would have guessed?"

Dr. Acosta glanced at her new patient a second or so, enough to give him a nod before going back to her notes. "You're sweet, Franz, I can see that. I'm guessing you're a quiet guy, too. Maybe a boy who has many thoughts."

Franz didn't know what to say. He had told his Uncle Max, yes, he'd go to therapy. The boy wasn't sure what therapy was, exactly – "You talk about your feelings," his uncle said – and that sounded okay. He didn't want to get his uncle angry. What other relative would take care of him? Franz didn't think he *had* other relatives. Perhaps Uncle Max was like his father and would order him out of the house.

"Go, just go!" The boy imagined Max yelling. "And don't bother taking your things with you. You're not pulling any fast ones on me, let me tell you. I'll be selling your things to pay the rent that you owe me. Did you think all this was for free, Mr. Pity Me I'm An Orphan? Did you think your Uncle Max had a sucker's heart? Sucker's hearts are for women."

Franz's mind could cook up a tale. *Inventive*, was the word his teachers used in the notes they wrote on the back of his report card. His father called "inventive" a nice word for lying. "You telling teachers things that aren't true, son?" Karl Hoffmann would ask. Franz's mother liked to say being inventive was a positive thing and showed a creative mind.

How did these two people ever marry?

The boy pictured himself wandering the streets of this foreign city so many kilometers from home, this beautiful, crazy Havana, the people talking to him in a language that made no sense, the boy so alone and without money. Franz imagined the people of Havana behaving like the ones in the waiting room, yelling at each other and striking out with their fists. Cuba was a country of angry people, a country that enjoyed scaring anyone who wasn't one of them. But none of that bothered Franz as much as his Uncle Max.

Last night the boy had gone to the bathroom at the end of the hall. Two-thirty-five in the morning, he had to pee or explode. He was already fantasizing about his body parts scattered over the frayed carpeted hallway – a lung here, a kidney there. When Franz opened the door, he saw his Uncle Max sitting on the toilet, elbows on his knees, blue pajamas bottoms gathered about his ankles. The moon shimmered through the skylight and turned the room to shadows and silver. Max's bare legs and feet were no more than thick, dark bristles covering bones.

HIS FATHER'S DIARY

"Gregor could see what Grete had in mind, she wanted to take her mother somewhere safe and then chase him down from the wall. Well, she could certainly try it!'

– Metamorphosis

Callejon de Hammel
Havana

FRANZ HOFFMANN LAY under the white sheet of the strange new bed Uncle Max had bought especially for his arrival. A skinny knee propped up the sheet, a flashlight focused on his dead father's scrawled, handwritten diary, most sentences written in a downward slant.

> ... no one can escape this type of evil. It would be like escaping your fingerprints or the way you part your hair. And you will think, "But this is crazy, it's too surreal." You will go over your sins, the ones you remember, and you will say, "Why is this happening to me?' As if you have forgotten a major crime somewhere, the one that would make the evil into an understandable thing.

Franz stopped reading for a moment. I shouldn't be such a coward, he thought. I'm supposed to ask questions. Poppa always expected that. He used to say, "This is what bright children do, they ask questions."

The boy imagined their conversation.

"So you've invaded my hideout," his father began, an eyebrow arched like Sam Spade with a new clue. "I don't know where to begin with you. You've disregarded my wishes and taken advantage of my trust. You've put a very big knife in my heart, Franz."

That arched eyebrow said more than any words. How many times had his father given people that look – to his son, to everybody – that "I know what you're up to" look. Nobody could fool him.

Then his father said, "Nothing's safe from your chronic prying. You'd make quite the detective, sonny boy."

Karl Hoffmann had never called him 'sonny boy' or given him such a big compliment. That didn't matter. Franz liked imagining a nicer father, a more sensitive and loving father, a man capable of at least an off-handed compliment.

Here was the joke, if you want to call it that: Franz didn't have an interest in the stupid diary. He'd skimmed it, mostly. Much of the diary was about his father's work. The boy remembered his mother saying, "God forbid a person should ask your father about his work. I don't know what's worse – your father telling me I wouldn't understand. Or him trying to explain it."

What Franz truly liked to do in his father's hideout was swivel the dark wood desk chair and roll the roll-top desk part up and down. He liked pretending he was a professor scolding students for not doing their studies properly.

"Do you wish to have a good, well-paying job?" he would say. "Money to raise a family, to send your own children to university? Or will you be a bum who sleeps in the streets and begs for food?" Franz would say these things with his father's stern face and voice. "Better watch yourself, young Roger. You too little Miss Abigail." Franz wasn't sure where he got the names Abigail and Roger, but these two were always "goofing off," as his father would say. "You can't goof off, and expect to succeed in this life."

Franz also liked looking at all the old timey photographs of the women in their shorts and puffy-sleeved T-shirts. When the boy visited his father's hideout, he felt close to him. He liked that feeling the best. He imagined so many things. His father sitting in the desk chair. His father writing in the small leather bound diary. His father protecting his own father's bathing beauties pictures. Franz vowed to always protect them, too. The bathing beauties, the diary, this perfect shadowy hideout with its smells of peppermint aftershave and, every so often, the leftover smell of pipe tobacco.

Mother hated any smell of tobacco in the house. She didn't understand how the tobacco smell could emanate from a bedroom closet.

"Have you been smoking in the closet?" she'd ask his father.

"Constantly," his father liked to say, a bit of a grin.

Two days before his parents were murdered, Franz discovered other photographs. These were black and white ones, men and women and children standing at attention. A full view and a side view – the type of photo police take when they arrest people. The pictures appeared more recent than his grandfather's bathing beauties collection. Franz had tripped over a raised board in the floor near the desk. He'd found these latest photos there. This particular loose board was on the shadowed side of the room, away from the removable wood panel that had allowed him to enter his father's hideout.

As Franz's went through the two dozen or so pictures, he felt his stomach start to knot and burn. A fiery sensation reached into him, that was the feeling, incomprehensible things working on his tummy, grabbing his breath.

"... what do I call you?" he had whispered.

The people in the photos had darker skin than the people he knew in Prague. They also had broad noses and wide foreheads. They were different in other ways, too. Each picture had reminded him of what he'd seen in carnivals, but nothing so simple as attached twins or bearded women. He would've understood attached twins playing musical instruments, or bearded women in evening gowns, their bright red mouths surrounded by hair.

That's why Franz and his family went to carnivals. They went to see the everyday freaks, the freaks they *expected* to see, freaks with no surprises, freaks who amused without shaking the world, the sort of people who quieted Franz's bad suspicions about himself.

The same printed words had been stamped on the back of each picture:

Property of Elijah C. Cummings
The Colony On the Padamo River
Venezuela

In the background of the pictures Franz could see three horseshoe shaped long houses nestled amid palms and shrubs and white sand. Each photograph had a different person in the foreground but all of them had some type of...his mother's word came to mind ... *condition*. A woman stood at attention, her bony arms half their normal size, the upper part of the arms fused to her sides. Another photo showed a young man whose limbs were covered in dark bristles.

There were many different conditions, some of

these conditions had actually changed the person into an entirely different thing – an insect, a beetle the size of a person. Did their changes only go one way? Did the people with the broad noses and wide foreheads stay beetles forever? Franz wanted to think the people in the photographs could shift back and forth between insect and human. The boy imagined himself becoming an insect with its black bristles, it's hard luminous shell, its bulging, oddly shaped eyes. He knew he didn't want to stay a beetle his whole life. Maybe they go back and forth, he thought. It wouldn't be too bad doing that.

Franz had taken the diary and the pictures of the colony from his father's hideout. But he'd left the bathing beauties in the desk drawer. He didn't understand why his grandfather had called them beauties.

SCREWING UP A SIMPLE THING

"It's true that you're under arrest, but that shouldn't stop you from carrying out your job. And there shouldn't be anything to stop you carrying on with your usual life."

– The Trial

In bed with Lottie and Aria
San Francisco de Paula

SHE DID HER best fretting in the dark. They were in bed, Aria and Lottie. Aria had forgotten her Breathe Rights again and her mouth was open and she kept making these startled guttural sounds Lottie could feel on the surface of her skin. Worse than chalk on a blackboard, Lottie thought, but she'd been letting it slide for close to an hour, the time now being 3:48 AM by the green digital clock on the nightstand. Who cares, she thought. There were far more important events conspiring to make their life into a living nightmare.

Lottie was reliving her afternoon conversation with her current contractor, Elijah C. Cummings, professional dick. He'd yet to deposit the agreed upon 75K. She'd been sitting on the front porch when she called him, an awning shading her. The noonday heat was rising from the street in front of her in rippling waves.

"I'm sorry, Mr. Cummings," she'd said. "Truly. But

I can't make this right without the money."

"...lesbian bitch." Elijah mumbling that one to himself.

"*Hey*, hey," Lottie had said, keeping it light but letting him know.

A month ago they'd met on South Beach at Boca Raton, Florida. He had said 1:00 AM, precisely. And she needed to sit in a beach chair that faced the ocean. His one rule was no looking back at him. If Lottie took a peek, she could kiss the job good-bye.

She didn't peek.

Yesterday afternoon Cummings was breathing in the phone like a fat man after dinner. He told her how he'd traveled thousands of miles to gather plants in a Venezuelan jungle for his pharmaceutical company. While searching the jungle with a coworker, he'd discovered a colony of people who were not quite regular. That was his word – "regular." People, he said, who were also something else. Half the time Lottie had no idea what the guy was saying; couldn't follow him. But she remembered thinking, he's going to make money off these people, these creatures.

"Let's talk about your fuck up," Cummings was saying. The man did an audible exhale as if his life would be so much simpler if he didn't have to concern himself with every type of bad shit in the known universe. "Let me get this straight. You killed your brother and his wife?"

"She was a nice person," Lottie said. "–Nice to me, anyway. I truly didn't want to hurt her, but she recognized me. You know, called me by name. I have a rule with husbands and wives. You can't kill one without killing the other."

"Ahh, okay, all right," Cummings said. "So a changed equation. You got a wife who calls you by name, recognizes you. I get it, what's an individual going to do? Still, the people I represent don't endorse – what would you call it – *darker* solutions."

"Who does, Mr. Cummings."

"My employers want to think of themselves as a family oriented company." The man's words were wrapped in steady breaths. "No scandals, that sort of thing. Like Caesar's wife. The pharmaceuticals industry thinks of themselves as the people who keep America healthy. But as you say, a person can't kill one without killing the other."

"I mean they *were* in bed together."

"Even worse – no escaping the inevitable," Cummings said. His talk was amiable enough but never *totally* amiable, that's how it felt to Lottie – amiable with a sinister edge. Then he said, "You got to think about loose ends."

"Truer words." Lottie couldn't disagree. She was listening to him while staring at a brief twirl of wind pick up the dust along the dirt road in front of her house. It weaved about like a miniature tornado.

"Your brother and I met in Seattle." Cummings said, "Extraordinary place Seattle, rains every other day, but a very clean city. We're there for a get together sponsored by my company. Your brother tells me how much he enjoyed my Venezuela presentation. 'Loved,' is the word he used. How he *loved* the photos I took of these genetic mutations. Your brother–"

"–*Step*-brother."

"Your step-brother thinks it's a 'romantic mystery.' Personally, I don't see it that way, but that's me. 'Outstanding photos,' Hoffmann says. So then he says he'd like to meet for drinks. You know, for a professional discussion. And would I mind bringing the photos for a closer peek." The malevolent meter on Cummings' whisper cranked up from a two to a four. "Are you getting the picture?"

"Not a surprise," she said.

"Your asshole step-brother stole my photographs." Cummings sounded embarrassed at his own naiveté. "Granted, we *were* drinking. The Hilton Bellevue has a great bar and a damn fine martini. The secret is the cinnamon. We drank several of those exquisite devils each – four, possibly five."

"Maybe the drinking part wasn't such a great idea," Lottie said.

"Nobody's kicking my ass more than me, darling."

"I want my money, Mr. Cummings."

"And I'm *ready* to give the money to you," he said, irritation riding the edge of his breath.

"These people trusted me, the people in the colony. And my company has pledged to make their situation better. But that's not your business. Your business to make things right. That's how you'll get your money."

NIGHT OF A REASONABLE MAN

"... oppressed with anxiety and self-reproach, he began to crawl about, he crawled over everything, walls, furniture, ceiling, and finally in his confusion as the whole room began to spin around him he fell down into the middle of the dinner table."

— Metamorphosis

Calle No. 15, the Vedado
Havana, Cuba

THE ENORMOUS BEETLE had settled itself on the dining room table. It was looking out the window at the three story sandstone brick apartments that lined either side of Callie 15 near the university. The Beetle called itself Cole, short for what he was, a Coleopteran. Cole enjoyed the palms and the fuzzy green shrubs cut just-so that decorated the courtyards, faculty housing for Max Hoffmann. The professor had opened the window earlier, anticipating the warm night and the damp breeze coming off Havana Harbor and from the spray of the waves hitting the seawall along the Malecón. The clear sky showed the moon and the many stars and turned the land and buildings into luminous silver.

Cole quivered and its smooth iridescent back split,

lifted and separated, its wings unfolding, quivering, wings made of cobwebbed silk. Its body trembled, the air on its wings gave a cool and glorious relief.

He could recall Max opening the dining room window but he didn't know how he had recalled it. Perhaps he *was* Max Hoffmann but in a different form. That thought had occurred to him many times, particularly when he awoke in, say, the living room instead of the dining room, or the bathroom instead of the bed. Cole had no idea how he'd gotten from one room into the other. He imagined himself in a continual metamorphosis, transitioning between this and that state and back again. The beetle could visualize Max with his dark bristled legs or the man's back becoming hard and iridescent. How could he do that unless he was Max or had been him before the change, the metamorphosis. Yet when Cole felt he was truly Cole, as he did now, he believed Max was someone or some*thing* very different, something apart from himself.

Maybe one day he'd stay Cole forever.

You mustn't let him see you, Cole thought. Now he was remembering the boy, Franz, walking into the bathroom two nights ago, big as you please, seeing his bristles, his dark thin legs. Cole was in mid-transition then but he remembered. Most of him was still Max Hoffmann, the professor seated on the toilet reading the *Havana Times*.

"You should always knock," Max said this to Franz in the kindest way.

The boy couldn't stop looking. "Were you in an accident? Is that it?"

"I have a condition." Max watched the boy; wondered how frightened boys his age got over answers vague enough to escape them. "Sometimes it's my legs. They get very thin and almost black. The little black hairs are dangerous. I've cut my fingers on them more than once. But sometimes my condition appears other places – my back, my chest, the thing's unsettling. And it gets worse, too. I have no control."

"Mother called it that," Franz had said, looking briefly at his bandaged hand. "She called it a 'condition.' I don't think people know what to call it, I know I don't. I'm always scared. I stay scared."

Max studied the boy, a second, two. And as if deciding a verdict, he'd said, "I think this will be very good for us. You and I, we can go through our conditions together. Let me tell you what I believe, my boy. Tragedies bring gifts, that's what I believe. I'm sure you wish you were home with your parents and everything was back to the way it was. The safe, the familiar. But God works in mysterious ways. Isn't that what people say? Do you believe in God, Franz?" His uncle didn't wait for an answer. "I find I go back and forth on the matter – one day yes, one day no. I am the proverbial black sheep, what can I say? My theologian friend tells me we are the ones God loves above all others – the black sheep. Maybe I'll stay a black sheep and get loved a lot. We are like a teaspoon of sugar in a sea of bitter greens. Or maybe God just likes a good challenge."

That's when Max told the boy to leave and shut the door.

Franz had done this right away; he didn't have to be told twice. The boy was more than ready, what his uncle thought. Nobody needed to see an old man who had bristled dark bones for legs. No sense scaring children half to death.

"Take a nice deep breath," Uncle Max said, his voice raised so his nephew could hear him on the other side of the shut door. "C'mon now, big breath. Let me hear you."

"I'm okay."

"You don't sound okay."

"You're legs..." Franz hesitated, his tone cautious. Then the boy knocked on the door gently and said, "Your legs are ... like my hand."

"Yes, the very same thing." Max flushed the toilet; stood and pulled up his gabardine slacks from about his ankles. He studied his face in the mirror a moment or two before saying, "Very clever of you to notice. Our afflictions come and go. No pattern that I can see – you know, the way an old person's toes or shoulders ache in rainy weather, or when our emotions are in an agitated state. You remind me of your father and me when we were your age."

"Will I get better?"

Max didn't answer his nephew's question. What could he say to ease the boy's fears, to ease his own? Instead Max went in another, safer direction, "These changes seem beetle-like to me. Beetles have the largest sub-species of any insect. Did you know that?" Max waited for the boy to perhaps ask another question, something he could answer. But there was only quiet. His uncle said, "It's true. Scientists think it's close to eight million. Can you imagine – eight million *types* of beetle? Amazing, isn't it? The Latin word is Coleoptera, my boy. It means sheathed wing. Did they teach you Latin in Prague? Do the schools do that nowadays, or is it too Catholic for them? They certainly did it in my time."

What else could one say, really?

The beetle was still lying on the dining room table, thinking about his time with the boy, imagining what his nephew would do if he knew the truth about his uncle. He enjoyed thinking about these scenarios. He'd been back and forth on it all – wanting him there, not wanting him.

But the boy was decent, a good boy, and they were kindred spirits, the boy and him, adventurers on the same bleak and winding road. There were other thoughts, too – equally pleasant ones. It had taken the beetle awhile to become good-natured enough to think of a name for itself.

Mr. Cole to you. Ha, ha.

MR. CUMMINGS

part 2

"... his condition seemed serious enough to remind even his father that Gregor, despite his current sad and revolting form, was a family member who could not be treated as an enemy."

– Metamorphosis

Heaven's Own
A gated community
Boca Raton, Florida

THE OLD WOMAN on the water resistant, floral lounge chair was looking at the pool and chatting with the old man, more an ongoing monologue than a give and take. Elijah C. Cummings was half listening and sipping his third totally dry martini – "I want the vermouth whispering to the vodka" – while the old woman drank a large, rose colored wine spritzer. He didn't know how many of those things she'd imbibed but one was more than enough to give a person diabetes.

"What did you say you did for a living?" the old woman wanted to know.

"Plants, snake oil and cure-alls, hon."

Elijah C. Cummings was a large man with enough flesh on him to stir the concern of strangers. How can he sleep with all that weight, how can he breath? One of many thoughts he'd guessed these strangers had about him. Other guessed at thoughts would be, think how hard his heart has to work. Or, he must be diabetic, too. And, yes, all that was true. He did have heart problems; he was diabetic. And diabetes brought its own set of problems, the chance of stroke, eye disease, nerve issues, wounds that failed to heal properly, malfunctioning kidneys. When Cummings thought about the possibilities, the many ways death could take him, he'd reach for a dose of comfort food, a couple of ninety-nine percent lean beef burgers, fries cooked in olive oil rather than lard, some butter pecan ice cream made with real pecans and cream made from cows who'd grazed on real grass and avoided sub-doses of antibiotics. No one could accuse him of not being health conscious.

"I pictured you more the west coast type," the old woman said. "–A producer, maybe, something along those lines."

"You have an imagination."

"My ex used to tell me that," the old woman said, her voice getting flirty. She gave Cummings a little poke in the bicep with a mint green painted nail. "Want to guess what I'm imagining now?"

"Listen, I'm gay. All right? Nothing I can do about it. I love my gayness. I thought I'd tell you that." Cummings wasn't gay. But this would stop shit before it got started.

The woman shifted direction without missing a breath. "So you sell cure-alls – what, like colds, arthritis, that sort of thing?" She had bronzed freckled skin and wrinkles about her neck and upper chest. She wore a shiny black one-piece bathing suit. Elijah thought the old gal's breasts could've been used for a water safety device. She said, "I desperately need something for my hay fever. My son who thinks with his dick and the new *shiksha* bitch he married literally kidnapped me from my townhouse in Philly and drove me here. Less

58

pollen, they said. Ms. *Shiksha* – heather, or Holly – kept shushing me every five minutes. Can you imagine? Never have a son whose middle name is Benedict Arnold."

"Biology and chemistry, that's what I do." Cummings said. "I don't *sell* anything."

"*Ah*, so a professional," she said. Cummings heard her voice perk up. Now she was really interested. "It isn't fair. Older men always look much more attractive than older women.

God is such a sexist, isn't he?" She didn't wait on a response. "Beatrice Klein," she said, and held out a limp manicured hand for him to shake or kiss or do with it whatever he wanted to do.

Cummings shook her fingertips, something perfunctory and non-lingering. "I'm surprised you don't own your own home," she said. "–College housing, perhaps. Isn't that what most of you geniuses do? Teach?"

"I find pharmaceutical projects for my company. Right now we're resolving a genetic mutation issue – you know, reversing the problem."

"Have mercy," Beatrice said, a tiny, apologetic giggle. "I'm only a community college gal – a semester of French, actually. My ex thought a trip to France would be nice. I hated to disappoint him. He counted on me for everything, you know. He thought we'd be the gracious Americans the French would finally like. Quiet, generous, fluent in their language. They're such difficult people to please. A lot like my ex, really. You can't imagine the pressure I felt about that trip."

Cummings ignored her chatter and said, "Think about it – what if your body was altering itself and there was nothing you could do? What would you pay to get yourself right again?"

"Now *that's* what I call fascinating."

"Yeah, a lot of us think that."

At first Cummings thought the old woman was only pretending fascination, the way some women do to show their interest in a man. Most men are too stupid to get that. But, no, this looked very genuine. "Everything in our environment can change us," he said. "–Our jobs, relationships, our politics. Believe me, we are altered in *many* ways, it's never just nature or nurture."

"...just fascinating," she murmured.

Beatrice Klein in Venezuela, wouldn't that be something? He smiled to himself at the thought of the woman in a pith helmet, batting away flies and mosquitos, sidestepping snakes while sweat and mascara rolled the length of her cheeks.

What would be her response as she looked through trees with their big mint green leaves, through an almost endless tangle of vine the width of your wrist, amid a burst of screaming birds, feathers everywhere, royal blue, bright yellow, a wild flash of red, what would she think and say as say as the secret little village came into view?

What would Beatrice Klein think of its inhabitants, Cummings wondered, some walking about and looking ordinary, some with faces, arms and legs in mid-transition, the bristles, the black bony limbs, the large, the dark protruding eyes. Others would already be in full form, of course, clinging to the sides of the huts, wings buzzing and shells drying in the noon heat.

Fascinating enough, sweetheart?

THE PRIVATE LIFE OF CORO ACOSTA

"… The way you brought me up, the weakness, the lack of self-trust, the guilt – all the things which put a cordon between me and marriage."

– Letter to My Father

La Habana Malecón
Havana, Cuba

CORO ACOSTA SAT in a white wicker chair, skinny brown legs crossed at the knee, looking at Havana Harbor and the *Bahia de la Habana* through binoculars. The breeze was warm tonight, the air damp from the bay. City lights shown silver and yellow on the water as the waves rushed the seawall and sprayed upward into the night.

I can't sleep," Coro whispered. "I need to people watch for awhile."

"Who's stopping you?" the ghost said. "Pretend I'm not here."

"You aren't here."

"So you say."

Dr. Acosta had a small apartment overlooking the Malecón and the wall. She'd lived there with her mother, Isabel, for close to seven years until her mother died in April. Now she lived there with her mother's ghost. Coro would see Isabel at the foot of her bed at night and down the shadowed hall that lead to the balcony. The psychologist believed the human brain was a meaning machine. That's what it did, it made sense of things, and this was what she as a new thirty-two year old orphan had to endure, a transcendent psychosis, nothing unusual – you cry, you don't sleep, you see the dead. The condition was temporary, the prognosis good.

"Did you always have those binoculars?"

"I bought them yesterday," Coro said.

"That's a positive sign." A cryptic ghost.

Young men and women were gathering along the pale stony edge of the seawall, teens, twenties, and they talked and laughed and some danced. Noisy evenings. Coro Acosta heard the music from the boom boxes and the cars that drove along the Avenida de Maceo. Time-warped Fords and Chevys and Desotos from the fifties and sixties. She loved these cars, cherry red, baby blue, always polished and pretty and driving easy like a parade. She wiggled her foot to the beat of the music.

"It's good I'm deceased," the ghost said.

"Don't bait me, mother."

"What do you mean 'bait'?' What is that?" Coro's mother was directly behind her. The daughter could smell the woman's gardenia perfume. Or thought she smelled it. "Psychology's an annoying profession," Isabel said. "You're always in everybody's business. Always blaming the mother. I'm just saying we can't take care of each other, anymore. How's that what-you-call baiting? Maybe now you'll find somebody."

Coro didn't miss her mother – okay, some days, maybe. She and Isabel had been together since Coro's father left them when she was a baby. But she didn't miss their talks about marriage.

"A woman should have a man," her mother's seven year mantra. Coro was a younger version of Isabel. Big eyes and coco skin, both were slim and looked young for their ages. The hair was different, no tight corn roll for the mother. Isabel's hair was long and white and thickly matted like a Rastafarian. "Just because your father left me – *us* – doesn't mean that will happen to you. A good man will protect the woman he loves," her mother had said. "A woman is a target for every dirty trick a man can dream up. Men are spies for the devil. Especially today, *mi querida*. Men see us as the meat. How do you say *pedazo de carne*?"

"–k Piece of meat."

"Sí, a piece of meat."

"Men aren't so important," Coro said, gave a little snort. "Can you picture me washing his socks? Or preparing *Ropa Viejsa*." 'Old clothes' in English, a dish of chewy stewed beef and vegetables. "Oh, and let's not forget caring for children; the day to day caring. I'm in awe of women who seem so easy with these tasks. Believe me, I'd swoon under the pressure."

"But you love children."

"I do, yes. You see how I worry about these poor babies who are not my own," Coro told Isabel. "Imagine me with my own little boy or girl – I'd be melted to the bone in a week, *madre*, less probably. I know my limits. I worry enough about the babies of strangers, I don't need my own sweethearts."

There were close to five hundred polyclinics throughout Cuba. Urban neighborhoods, rural towns. Each clinic served twenty-five or so families. Coro had an ever growing caseload of kids, none over the age of sixteen. Even a small case load of children was a *lot* of children.

She didn't need to go home to two or three of her own.

"See, you *do* need a life," Isabel whispered. Coro glanced behind her at the open glass doors leading to the balcony. Nobody there, thank you, Jesus. But a person can never be too sure. She lifts her binoculars to check out the young people on the wall. Her dead mother said, "That's what fun looks like, in case it slipped your mind. Sexy boys and sexy girls dancing to very sexy music."

"–Okay, mother."

"Do you remember how to dance, *estimada*?"

"I was very popular," Coro whispering to herself now. "But I've responsibilities. I have my studies – or had them – and I definitely had you."

"Don't blame me," Isabel said, annoyed now.

"No. no, *madre*. These were my choices." Dr. Acosta was surprised at the anxiousness in her voice. She felt weary just hearing her own words.

Coro said, "We accommodate life. Everyone chooses all the time; my choices are mine. Nobody's blaming–"

Dr. Acosta stopped. She'd focused her binoculars to get the best view of the seawall and saw him right off – her client, my God, her *client*, twelve year old Franz Hoffmann.

But who was he with?

Children needed to be careful nowadays. Gangs roamed the streets. They'd grab a kid and put a gun in his or her hand and tell them to go murder the kid's family or murder a person the kid didn't know. That's what was going on today. If kids wanted to belong to a gang, they would do as they were told. Oh, Coro knew about these gangs, these stupid boys and girls. Everybody here knew a lot more than they used to know. Cuban people bought news and sports packages for their computers. They watched soccer games and learned about the new wars. They watched crazy Americans shoot anything they wanted to shoot. Americans wore weapons to shop for groceries. Illegal satellite dishes appeared on the roof tops in Havana, maybe for a week, maybe a month, longer, depending on the cleverness of the owner. No government could stop the curiosity of a person. Closed Cuba was becoming more open to what was going on in the world.

"Who are you watching?" her mother's ghost said.

"–Nothing." Coro Acosta was still looking through her binoculars.

"You can't fool me." Isabel said, a breath on Coro's cheek.

The boy's companion was an older woman. Forties, perhaps early fifties, it was hard to tell. The woman's dark hair frizzed out and covered her shoulder and ended at the middle of her back. Coro had mistaken two spiked points of hair for ears. She'd never seen so much hair. The older woman wore black Spandex bike pants and a sleeveless black Spandex pullover. The hair covered her thin arms, too. They were talking, Franz and the woman, then out of nowhere she slapped the boy's face.

STEP-AUNTIE

"His mother would point to Gregor's room and say, "Close that door, Grete," and then, when he was in the dark again, they would sit in the next room and their tears would mingle..."

— Metamorphosis

THE WOLF LADY was skinnier than Franz had thought. She'd slapped him hard across the face and shook his shoulders with both hands. He felt the sting on his cheek. The woman had on a sleeveless Spandex top, and the dark hair on her arms was there but it wasn't as thick and glossed as it looked at a distance. Franz could see her pale skin beneath the hair, the hard muscle and tendons.

She shook him again.

"–Where?" she whispered, more a hiss, her brownish gold eyes glaring at him. She had introduced herself as his Auntie, his *step*-auntie, telling him that his father had stolen photos from her friend and she wanted them back and she knew her brother had them – her *step*-brother.

"You tell me, boy, or I'll shake your teeth from your head. Do you believe me? You want me to do that?"

Franz shook his head, quickly, emphatically. "No, ma'am, no I-I don't." She hadn't released his shoulders. He said, "Please, auntie. You're hurting my arms."

The Wolf Lady leaned toward him. "I'll break both your puny arms, boy," she said. "Your hideous daddy didn't have the scruples God gave him. Here's a family fun fact: when we were children – a bit younger than you – the little shit used to torture me. A snake in the bed, a match to the hem of my skirt. Once he tied me to a tree and left me in the woods overnight. Your daddy was a regular jokester. And God forbid I'd threaten to tell mother. Then he'd say, 'Oh c'mon, Lottie, it was joke. Can't you take a joke?' Are you like that – like dad like son? Is that you, boy?"

"No, ma'am." Franz felt his stomach tighten.

"Good, very wise." His auntie was stroking his cheek with the back of her hand, the fingers warm, her voice soft and gentle, almost sweet. "Because abuse like that can't go unpunished. That wouldn't be appropriate; wouldn't be fair. And I let your daddy know my feelings. That night I got a golf club from your grandfather's bag in the hall closet – just the putter, a small club. Your father was asleep when I hit him. If I remember right, the putter struck Karl's left cheek. It shattered the bone. But you know how those sorts of things go. You're a young man of the world. I knocked him right off the bed. Blood was everywhere, or that's how it seemed at the time – blood on the sheets, the walls, the wood floor."

The boy tried again to twist free. "I'm not like that, I'm not a thief."

"Oh I think you're very much a thief." She held his chin with a thumb and forefinger, moving his face right to left profile. "I know a thief when I see him. What's the expression? 'It takes one to know one' – have you heard that?" She didn't wait for an answer. "Like most expression, it's got a bit of truth. Your old auntie can smell a bad boy like some people can smell a storm coming."

"I-I stole coins from my *matka's* purse once," he said, using the Czech word for mother. "I-I wanted a pastry. I told her, though. I paid the coins back, I swear."

"A thief with a conscience is a bad thief." His auntie grinned, two of her upper teeth looked bigger and more yellowed than the others. Franz felt the pressure of her grip relax, but the woman didn't let go of his shoulder completely. She leaned her face closer to him, audibly inhaling the scent of his hair and whispering, "I'd advise taking up a less guilt ridden occupation."

"I will, Auntie. I-I promise."

She knelt in front of him, eye level. "You know about the photographs. Don't you, boy, you know."

A wave hit the seawall and it's tall spray showered down on them. Droplets glittered in the lights of passing cars and nearby restaurants. Two teenage girls who sat on the seawall not too far from Franz and his auntie got sprayed, too. They squealed and laughed, jiggling their arms.

"I saw the pictures once, a long time ago," Franz said. He'd imagined himself calling out to the two girls or maybe the others that were taking a night stroll along the seawall but he feared his auntie would read his mind before he could get the words out of the mouth. "I don't know when I saw them, months, maybe."

"And what did little Franz see?" The Wolf Lady watched his face, her brown gold eyes on the look out for clues. "Tell auntie."

"People, that's all."

"Just people?"

"People, you know –" Franz wasn't sure what he could or couldn't tell her and remain safe. "–People ... like me," he said and raised his bandaged hand.

"Of course, I should have known. Poor dear nephew." She lifted his wrist and examined the white gauze. Franz thought she was going to kiss his hand the way his mother used to do. But auntie surprised him. She sniffed it ever-so-briefly. His auntie said, "Unless I get what I want, the people in those photos will come for you. Let me rephrase that, the *things* in those pictures will come for you. Am I understood, boy?" Franz nodded slowly. "Is that something you'd like? Do you want those things hiding in your closet or under your bed?"

Before Franz had a chance to answer, he glanced up and noticed a woman running toward them. She was thin and dark and had corn rolled hair.

LIFE AT THE COLONY
part 1

"... he was covered in the dust that lay everywhere in his room and flew up at the slightest movement; he carried threads, hairs, and remains of food about on his back and sides; he was much too indifferent to everything now to lay on his back and wipe himself on the carpet..."

– Metamorphosis

Spring
Puerto Ayacucho, Venezuela

THE RIO ORINOCO will shift on you, Cummings had said this many times. It's 1,700 miles expanded and contracted as if it constantly needed to breathe. He'd rented a longboat with a small outboard motor. His carrier, guide and translator, Javier, steered the narrow boat through the intricate twists of the rainforest. Javier had dark skin and blue eyes – the father a passing Dutch trader – and he was thin enough to have countable ribs. Squirrel monkeys watched them from the shoreline, jumping and twirling in the white sand, making angry noises to frighten them away. Parrots were everywhere, especially the multi-colored McCaws and the yellow-headed ones with green wings, the forest was alive with birds.

Cummings had gone there looking for pharmaceuticals with his biologist friend Harriet Fine, who worked for the same company but in the drug research division in Tallassee.

"I'm going to cure cancer, Eli." That's what she'd said when he first met her, three years ago now. Everything about Harriet was severe, her gray black hair pulled tightly into a bun, her sharp nose and chin, her white now sunburned pink skin stretched about the muscle and the bone. On their trip she wore a floppy tan hat and an excessive amount of sun guard. The other thing about Harriet Fine: the woman couldn't tell a joke if she tried. Cummings knew her well enough to know that. Harriet had only one speed – very serious. Most of that seriousness was about her cancer research. "I'm working on an immunotherapy treatment for cancer patients," she'd say. "When some cancer patients get an infection, their immune response is strong enough to kill both the infection and the cancer. And it doesn't seem to matter what *type* of cancer – it's dead, it's gone. So what I'm looking for is a plant that can induce an immune response without having the patient go through an infection. This jungle is the place to find that plant, Elijah. You're looking at the biggest drug store in the world."

That was No Nonsense Harriet Fine. On the second day of their jungle hike, the humidity close to unbearable, Cummings had watched Harriet part the heavy vines and foliage with the tip of her machete. Whatever she saw had stolen the color from her face and left her mouth open.

"God, look," she had whispered.

"You okay?" He wasn't sure what was going on.

What Elijah Cummings saw rattled him, too. A section of rainforest had been cleared, the trees used to build four large barrack-like structures that

surrounded a communal area where villagers could hold meetings and prepare and cook food, what tribal people did. But this wasn't any tribe Cummings had ever seen. There must have been 150, maybe 200 individuals. Multiple ethnicities, that was obvious from the first look. A third of the group belonged elsewhere, Europe
maybe, the U.S., India, perhaps Pakistan, certainly Asia – Elijah Cummings had no way of actually knowing, not then, not from a brief peek through jungle shrubbery.

What he saw at first were bodies in various stages of disarray. "Transformation," the word Harriet used. Some had dark limbs slender as twigs and covered in what ... fur, tiny quills? Their heads were in the process of reshaping themselves. Cummings couldn't see the changes in real time. The ones further in the process had long oval faces with extended foreheads and silvery black honeycomb eyes. Scabs had replaced the hair on their heads, the beginning of a slick reflective shell. The beginning of the same type of shell clung to their shoulders and back. They reminded Cummings of June bugs, the identical iridescent green. Individuals who'd transformed completely clung to the sides of the buildings or lay on the flat, thatched roofs. Some who were still in the throws of the metamorphosis lay on their sides, twitching. A few squealed in pain.

This was a colony bound by a single affliction, Cummings understood that from the start, but there were also people who watched, people like him, perhaps the ones who'd turned back to their human state. It's like a village of lepers, he thought, half expecting to see Mother Teresa descended from heaven and bathing the feet of these creatures.

"I've seen people like these in some of the bigger cities," Harriet said, her voice barely audible. She stood

next to Cummings, looking through the foliage. "–
Mumbai, London. I saw one on the subway in New
York. He wore a hoody, but I saw those terrible scabs
on his face, the beginning of those eyes. Everything else
about him was normal. I thought it was a birth defect,
something logical, something ordinary. In a way, it's a
form of cancer, isn't it? All these rogue genes. Jesus,
Elijah, we're looking at a damn epidemic."

WHAT STRANGER TO TRUST

"You're a keen observer," said K., "for between you and me I'm not really powerful. And consequently I suppose I have no less respect for the powerful than you have, only I'm not so honest as you and am not always willing to acknowledge it."

– The Castle

"I *SAW* YOU," Coro said to the woman who was still holding Franz by his shoulder. Coro had been breathing hard from her run. "You *hit* this child, this boy, I saw you do it. He's under my care, assigned to me by the state – *my* responsibility. What gives you the right to do such a thing? Do you always go around smacking little boys?"

"I'm *not* a little boy," Franz said.

"I happen to be his auntie," the woman said.

Coro wanted to tell the woman that she didn't look like anybody's auntie. Aunties don't have wild gypsy hair, and they don't dress in black Spandex like bicycle racers. Aunties are sweet and caring and wear sensible clothes. But Coro knew relatives came in every size and shape and mental condition. A day didn't go by that she didn't have to peel this one off that one in her clinic, trying to set them straight, telling them how differences weren't always settled with fists and shouts. They, of course, stared at her like *she* was the crazy person.

The doctor knelt on one knee, eye-level with Franz. "Are you all right?" She wanted to know, touching his hair, looking at the fading hand print on his right cheek where his auntie had slapped him. "You don't have to stay here, okay? You can come with me. I can walk you home, Franz. Do you understand?"

"The boy is fine," his auntie said.

"He doesn't look fine." Dr. Acosta glanced up at the woman. "I *know* fine, okay? This isn't it. This is a boy who's scared to death." Then to Franz, ""You can come with me, pal. The choice is yours. I'll walk you back to your uncle's place, okay? Is your Uncle Max home?"

"He's asleep," Franz said, his voice soft, maybe embarrassed.

"I used to sneak out, too. Got to have some fun, right?"

The boy smiled to himself.

"You need to leave," the auntie said.

Coro ignored her, this woman with the hair, this gypsy, this child beater. Coro spoke directly to Franz; a little to the auntie, too. "I may seem small, but you've been in my waiting room at the clinic, yes? So you know I'm a very tough girl, right? I'm busting up fights everyday. Big guys, too. Big guys with big muscles – they don't bother me. My daddy taught me how to fight. Did you ever hear of Anton The Crucifier Acosta?"

The boy shook his head. But he was definitely listening. What kid didn't like a good story about a guy named The Crucifier?

Coro keep on, "No? Seriously? One of the *great* Cuban wrestlers, maybe the *greatest.*"

Franz smiled, tentative, but a smile nonetheless. Dr. Acosta knew he was listening and she said, "My daddy was a legend, pal, you ask anyone. Fifteen minutes, that's all it took for him. And they went down, everyone who challenged him. They called my dad the

Fifteen Minute Man. Women would swoon and men would run. They all knew Anton."

"For*get* this," the auntie said, pissed now, no question about it.

"We're not finished here," Coro told her, but still looking at the boy and smiling.

"This is family business." Franz's auntie hadn't let go of him.

People strolled along the walkway next to the seawall and cars were moving slowly up and down the avenue. Headlights cut yellow knives into the night, their radios at full volume. Coro saw the woman's thumb and index finger press tighter into the boy's shoulder. The doctor pretended the auntie wasn't there. Win the child and you win the war, she thought. And Coro said, "Let me tell you about Gimoaldo the Giant, the day he came to our little village, Franz. What do you say?" She didn't wait for an answer. "I was a girl then, maybe eight or nine, I don't know, but a baby girl – and Gimoaldo seemed like Goliath in the bible. You know Goliath?"

The boy nodded, watching her now, his eyes big and dark. Coro loved that; loved the way kids craved a good story. She said, "Gimoaldo walked about our village, his every step trembling the earth. '*Where* is this Crucifier?' he'd shouted. 'Where is this infant disguised as a man?' Well I'd never seen anyone so big. How can daddy stop a giant? I remember thinking. He's half Gimoaldo's size. The fight is so unfair. I began to fear for my daddy's life. Tears filled my eyes and rolled down my cheeks. I did not want to lose my brave, sweet daddy. If the giant kills him, who'd protect me? Who'd bring my mother and me the money to buy our food and clothes? Who'd bring me pastries and surprises?"

"What nonsense," the auntie said. "Do you expect

anyone to believe–"

The boy interrupted her. "Where was he, your father? He didn't sound like the type who'd run."

"You are absolutely, one hundred percent correct, Franz." Coro touched the boy's cheek with her fingertips. "Daddy fell on Gimoaldo from the roof. He'd climbed to the highest roof in the village and waited for the giant to pass under him."

"I knew that," the boy said, nodded to himself.

"He looked so little on the giant's shoulders," Coro said. "–Like a boy on a mountain.

But everyone in the village cheered my father. 'Take him, Crucifier!" they shouted. 'Bring him to his knees!' they shouted. That day Gimoaldo the giant flung my father off him time after time.

The morning became the afternoon, and my father climbed back onto the giant's shoulders again and again. The people in our village continued cheering him on. 'Go Crucifier!' they shouted.

'Take him!' they said. I was afraid the fight would never end."

"Did he win? Your father, did he kill the giant?"

"Yes, he did. Of course, he did." Coro kissed the boy's forehead. "That's my whole point, Franz. Little people can win, too. Little people can be strong and fearless."

BUGS THAT SCARE US

"... It is as if one man had five low steps to walk up, and the second man had just a single step, but the single step was as tall as the five put together..."
— Letter to My Father

Karl celebrates his son's birthday
Prague

THE DAY AFTER Franz's sixth birthday, Karl Hoffmann locked his son in the kitchen pantry with a dozen or so Black Vine Weevils from his nocturnal collection. Franz pounded the door with his fists, pleading for his freedom. Every so often he would shout for his mother to intervene in what his father kept calling a "birthday surprise." Karl sat on the wood floor with his back to the pantry door and discussed beetle facts with his boy as he drank the half bottle of chardonnay he'd found in the refrigerator.

"...please, daddy," Franz said.

"There are twenty-five thousand different Coleoptera in North American," his father said. "Can you imagine that, boy? All different, all unique – the simple beetle. And we haven't begun to discuss the world wide population. Boggles the mind, doesn't it?"

"Poppa, I-I'm scared," Franz whispered.

"Of course you are, any sane person would be scared. There are days when those numbers terrify me.

79

And *I'm* a grown man. I'm a logical, *prac*tical man, Franz, a man not given to the hysterics of girls and wives – *or* little boys." Karl had just struck a match to the bowl of his pipe and began sucking the stem to ignite the tobacco. His wife was on a two day trip, visiting her sister. Karl liked smoking his pipe in the house when his wife wasn't there. The bluish white smoke swirled about his head. He shook the match out, blew on it and dropped it into the pocket of his denim shirt. He said, "The world changes us, Franz. Do you know what I mean by that – how the world changes us?"

"Let me out, poppa. Please, I'll behave, you'll see."

"A person needs to feel in control, Franz. Concentrate on what I'm saying. We all need to see ourselves as masters of our fate. The more we don't feel that way, the more we fall apart."

He took the pipe from his mouth and looked down at the bowl, tapped at it with his index finger. Smoking this thing shouldn't give a man so much trouble, Karl thought and sucked on the stem audibly. A bit of smoke curled out of the bowl. He leaned his hand over his right shoulder and knocked on the closed pantry door. "It's true, even the best of us fall apart. Presidents and kings. Wise men and fools. Here's the issue, Franz, we need to feel protected in this world. That's the long and the short of it. And when we don't feel protected, we get very nervous. Does that make sense to you?"

"...yes, daddy."

"Then you see how safe a beetle must feel, yes?"

"I-I don't know, daddy." Franz's voice had a tremble to it. "I don't know beetles. Do they bite? I had to brush one off my leg. Do they hurt people?"

"See, you're already missing my point." Right now Karl's pipe was working good, a nice steady draw, and he stopped his conversation with the kid to enjoy the

moment – a man and his pipe, relaxing here in the
kitchen and having a little *tête-à-tête* with his son.
What father would not find such an event rewarding?
None, he'd bet, positively none. "But that's all right,"
Karl said. "What we have here is a teachable moment.
To answer your question, the beetles keeping you
company aren't biters. If you think about it, Franz,
this is very clever. I've placed you in a situation that
forces you to *feel* them. Hell, forces me to feel *you*
feeling them. Do you feel them, Franz, the beetles, our
Black Vine Weevil friends?"

"They keep crawling on my legs," Franz said.

"Good. How do they feel, the beetles?"

"I dunno ... hard."

"Ah, ex*act*ly."

Karl took another swig from the bottle of cold
chardonnay. A man needed to relax, he thought. The
world had become too emotionally crippling not to take
advantage of exotic, mind comforting substances, no
question about it. The drug problem wasn't a problem.
The fucking world was the problem, the drug problem
was the cure. Yesterday one of his students, Elaina
Pavolovsky, a beautiful child with the longest most
stunning legs he'd ever seen – Elaina with blond hair
like Rapunzel – hair so magnificent he would've
wrapped his cock in that hair and ejaculated until he'd
passed out and died – Elaina Pavolovsky had paid three
classmates five hundred dollars a piece to deeply
perforate her lovely body with knives.

"Yes, poppa, you're right." Franz's voice had
become louder. A bit more manic, Karl thought. "Yes,
yes, poppa – beetles have *very* hard shells, hardest
shells ever."

"This is why the beetle has been with us for
millions of years," his father said. "Can you imagine?
The beetle was here before we were here and the beetle

will be here after we are dead and rotting. What does that tell you, boy?"

"What do I say, poppa?"

"You say what you think," Karl said. He was sitting cross-legged now and gazing out the kitchen window. A heavy feeling had flooded into his chest and shoulders. He'd had this feeling before and didn't know why. Karl felt tears at the edges of his eyes but he didn't want to cry in front of his son. It didn't matter than his son was in a pantry with the door closed. "–Always that," Karl said. A person must say what he thinks. Why ask such a question? And never let others put words in your mouth."

Silence.

"...Franz? You still with me?"

"Shells make them safe?" The boy's tone soft, hesitant.

"Wow, look at you. Outstanding."

A 12:16 AM RETURN

"Your question, my Lord, as to whether I am a house painter – in fact even more than that, you did not ask at all but merely imposed it on me – is symptomatic of the whole way these proceedings against me are being carried out."

– The Trial

Max Hoffman's Townhouse
Havana

DR. ACOSTA WAITED for Franz to unlock his uncle's front door. He waved to her before going inside and she waved back. The boy watched her from the bay window in the living room as she turned and walked through the shadows and moonlight. Franz thought about how Dr. Acosta had told his auntie to take her hands off him or she would call the police. There was a no nonsense something in the doctor's voice, what she used in the waiting room of her clinic to break up fights before they got worse, and he'd felt his auntie's fingers relax enough to wiggle his shoulder free.

"Don't look back," Coro Acosta had whispered to him. Noisy waves broke into spray on the seawall behind them. Talk and laughter and the music from radios were part of the night, too. Franz felt the doctor 's hand pushing him gently along. Acosta was looking straight ahead when she told him, "I need you to keep up, okay? We want to leave before your auntie thinks of a reason to show me her shit – I mean her angry feelings."

"I say 'shit.' I'm not an infant, you know."

"Okay. Her shit then."

Franz stayed at the bay window, a brief smile at a corner of his mouth at what Dr. Acosta had said, the part about the Wolf Lady not showing her shit, saying it like he was a grown up, an equal. He couldn't see the doctor now. She'd disappeared into the night, but that didn't matter. Franz liked recalling what she had done, how she stood up for him.

"Where have you been?" Uncle Max was behind Franz.

"I ... I couldn't sleep," Franz said and squinted into the darkness of the living room. He saw his uncle was holding a pistol, the sort of pistol the police use on TV shows – what the TV police called "snub-nosed." The boy said, "Are you going to shoot me?"

Uncle Max looked down at the pistol. "I thought you were a burglar."

"It's dangerous to point a gun at somebody."

Max looked at the weapon then placed it on the small table next to his pale blue velour recliner. "So you leave without saying anything? You don't leave me a note, something?"

"I didn't want to burden you," Franz said.

"You going out at night *is* a burden."

"I won't do it again, Uncle. I promise."

Max stepped into the moonlight and began hobbling toward him. He had on white boxers and a sleeveless-t. What Franz noticed first was his uncle's skin, pale and angled by bone. The man had the look of a holocaust survivor. Max's legs were different than when Franz had accidently seen him sitting on the toilet. Gone were the dark bristles; the feet that were

84

not quite feet, anymore. Tonight his legs appeared white washed, legs with no meat. How could he stand on those things? Franz wondered. The man used a blond wood cane and had a silver brace on his left leg. The brace was a size too big and it made a metal on metal noise when he moved.

"You look frightened," Max said. "I am getting better now. You'll see, nephew. Already my color is returning, the shape of my legs. Amazing, isn't it?" Max was the scientist now, viewing himself with curiosity "I wanted to show you how it happens, the ebb and flow of our condition. We are never lost for very long, Franz. Don't you see? We are stubborn and strong, you and I – all of us. We're fighters, you should remember that."

This morning his uncle had cleaned the boy's misshaped hand and wrapped it in a new bandage. Franz's hand hadn't improved, nothing about it looked better than yesterday or the day before yesterday. If anything it looked worse. His fingers were gone, or a person couldn't see the differentiation of the palm ending and the fingers beginning. Everything was fused together, a solid, oddly shaped mass, closer to a thin, longish hook. The skin had become darker, maybe not as dark as his uncle's legs but darker than the skin on his arm. Bristles were beginning to sprout to the rear of the hook the way some gloves had fur about the cuff.

"I'm not getting better," Franz said.

"You will, dear." Uncle Max placed his fingertips beneath the boy's chin, lifting his face slightly and looking into his nephew's eyes. "There are tricks to getting better."

"Mama gave me different medicines," Franz said. "Six or seven different ones – pills, lotions. She soaked my hand in chemicals that you mix with water. But nothing helped. It just irritated my skin, mostly; made everything itch or burn. I don't think there are any tricks. After a while, mama stopped telling me it would get better. She'd given up on me. I started feeling like I'd never get my hand back. I'm ashamed to say it but I began to believe mama wasn't a doctor at all, or at least she wasn't a good doctor."

"Your mother was a *very* good doctor," Max said.

"Good doctors heal people."

"This isn't about medicines." His uncle eased himself onto a small gray corduroy sofa then patted the cushion next to him. Franz sat down, elbows propped on his knees, looking at the wood floor. Max said, "People may tell you it's about medicines, the right drug, not that your mama didn't know how to help people who had infections and broken bones. But none of your bones look broken to me. I'm guessing you don't have an infection? No cuts, no viral stuff? Am I right?"

"...just my hand." The moment Franz mention the hand it began throbbing. The hand, or whatever it was, or whatever it was becoming, loved to tease him; loved making itself known. "I feel like my hand is the boss. It wears me out."

"Knowledge is always king, nephew." Uncle Max patted Franz's back. He did it tentatively, perhaps not sure how one soothed a child. "When we finally know what something is, that thing, that awful thing, it will never hurt us in the same way again."

ARIA GOES TO CONFESSION

"And how was I prepared for this? As badly as possible. Which I'm sure is already clear. You didn't involve yourself in any personal instruction..."
— Letter to My Father

Iglesia de San Francisco de Paula
San Francisco de Paula

"WHEN WAS YOUR last confession?"

Already Aria felt guilty. "...I dunno, Father."

"Well, that's not good."

"Yeah, tell me about it." Aria Maloof thought of herself as a lapsed Catholic. She'd left Egypt close to the end of her 10th year but even then she knew Catholics and Muslims despised one another and most believed a knife in the chest of the other was far too compassionate. Aria didn't trust or care for religion – the comfort a person found there wasn't worth the bloodshed one had to endure. She said, "I know I have 'spiritual issues', Father. But those must wait for another time. Right now I have to resolve a terrible problem."

"The church is always here for you."

The confessional smelled of oak and varnish, and the small slat and wire screen window showed the broken shadow of the priest's head. If Aria had not seen Father Jorge's tall, stooped presence in the market and

narrow dusty streets of the town, she wouldn't have guessed he was a man in his late sixties. His voiced sounded late thirties-early forties. He had good language skills, too. Spanish was his main language, of course, but she also thought he spoke decent
English. Once she'd even heard the man giving directions to a tourist in French.

Now it was time to get down to it.

"I have ... a friend," Aria said, her tone cautious. She stopped; then decided to go with her thought. "For years, I've ignored the questionable side of this friend. What some would describe as the 'darker side.' You understand?"

"Just say what's in your heart."

"But do *you* understand what I'm saying?"

"I've been doing this for awhile," the priest said.

"I'll take that as a 'yes.' Should I do that?"

"You have my attention."

I guess that'll have to do, Aria thought. She said, "I've ignored many things over the years with my friend. Many things she's done are things I question. My friend isn't the easiest person to get along with, so talking about certain issues might cause disastrous results. I could lose her forever, conceivably. But in my defense, let me say, I'm no dummy. I also know she would be lost without me. And if I'm honest, I, too, would be lost."

"It's good to have someone to love."

"It is, Father, yes."

"Yet..." Father Jorge said, and paused.

She hated people who did that – the 'yet' people, the 'but' people. Maybe 'hate' was too strong a word. "Okay, Father, I'll wait. Collect your thoughts."

"I'm just musing here," the priest said.

"Uh-huh. Muse away."

"Don't we lose that special person when we feel we

can't say those important things? Don't we ourselves grow distant from the ones we love? In other words, don't we lose them, anyway?"

Okay, not too lame, she thought. "That could happen, yes."

"It's a terrible chance we take." Father Jorge coughed, the sound wet and phlegmy. Aria wondered if the guy was getting ready to keel over on her. But he quit the cough and cleared his throat, managing to say, "There are no guarantees, are there? That's what we want – the guarantee, a safe road for the difficult things."

"I'll admit to that, Father."

"Good, that's half the battle, maybe three quarters."

"I always try being brutally honest with myself," Aria said. Immediately she felt the "brutally" part was overkill.

"When we say what's in our heart, we don't know how it'll be received." Father Jorge peered at her through the slats of the confessional window. She caught him doing it. He turned from her and continued, "We're anxious that we will lose the loved person. Isn't it far better, we think, not say anything at all, to keep our feelings and thoughts to ourselves? But let me tell you, sooner or later the heart betrays us. Who can stop a heart from going after what it wants? We can only pretend we're not involved. So either you do what needs to be done, or the heart will do it for you. Either you will look inward and understand your goal, or your heart will tire of you and sweep you away."

"I'm afraid for my friend's soul," Aria said.

"Then you must help her."

"It's not that easy."

"And here we are, back at square one," Father Jorge said. "See how it works?"

Aria's eyes had adjusted to the darkness of the confessional. She attempted to squint beyond the slats and screen of the small window. She saw the priest's white buzz cut, the unimpressive chin, a nose that dominated his narrow face, not the sort of man who gathered much attention.

"No, no," Aria said, shaking her head. "I'm serious, it's *really* not that easy."

"Helping a loved one can be difficult, but not impossible."

Coming to see Father Jorge had been a very bad idea. It shows how desperate you've become, she thought. You cannot put this priest in danger. What would you do then? Lottie is a person who crosses her "t"s and dots her "i"s, you know that.

"Señorita Maloof? Are you there?"

Two days ago Aria had gone to the San Francisco de Paula library to use the computer. She'd done a search that took her to the Prague Post, one of the more popular online newspapers in Lottie's home town. One prominent story was the double murder of a couple that lived near the Old Town Square, Karl and Judita Hoffmann. They'd been reading in their bed when an intruder had entered the room and shot each of them in the forehead.

"... Señorita Maloof?"

"People kid themselves," Aria said. "You must know that, Father. We do it all the time. People daydream their lives away, as if they're in a restaurant selecting the good parts of a bad meal. The *unlucky* ones – the ones like me – we wake up to the world as it is, a world too scary to imagine."

THE COLONY
part 2

"… for the days that I have been living here I will, of course, pay nothing at all, on the contrary I will consider whether to proceed with some kind of action for damages from you, and believe me it would be very easy to set out the grounds for such an action."
– Metamorphosis

Puerto Ayacucho, Venezuela

THE BEETLES HAD neither accepted or rejected Elijah C. Cummings and his biologist friend, Harriet Fine, nor did they have opinions on the couple's pharmaceutical hunt. And beetles were everywhere – human-sized beetles, either fully formed or partially formed – a mandible, a long claw hook, a green luminous shell. There were people, too, and Cummings talked to many of them. Most were from towns in Venezuela, but there were also Europeans and Americans. They looked worn and not just worn but catastrophically worn. They reminded him of Sisyphus hauling the rock, a haunted glaze to his eyes. He guessed they'd recently returned from their beetle metamorphosis.

Elijah was having trouble catching a full breath, the jungle humidity overwhelming. Who in their right mind would live here? The community reminded him of F.D.R.'s long ago polio retreat – before Cummings' time, of course – but he'd seen documentaries, Franklin's despair, his expectation of a cure slowly tattered, lost to an unforgiving change. Polio had its own mind and there was no cure then. Roosevelt could find no path back to dancing the two step, or playing croquet with his boys, or riding the ponies with Anna. What was left was Franklin's sizable will, his rage at an injustice that would never recognize his privilege.

Why beetles, though, Cummings thought. An odd virus perhaps, the new AIDS? Or a cancer, maybe Harriet Fine was right. How do these plights appear, these potential extinctions? What tweak in the ecosystem? It could be anything, a diet of fast foods and bad chemicals, oceans with their ten mile string of garbage and plastic bags, industries contaminating the rain forests, even some extraterrestrial fiend riding the back of a meteorite – a little surprise from God? *Or*. Here was his speculation at full tilt: had evolution just taken a weird turn to protect the species? That hard, luminous shell, Cummings guessed. Isn't that what we've always needed? Drop a beetle from the roof of a building and it walks away.

Didn't we always need the shell?

His biologist colleague, Harriet, had just told a beetle she was from Florida State in Tallassee.

The beetle answered her. Cummings heard the thing, and he saw Harriet heard it, too.

But the beetle hadn't spoken out loud. The words simply appeared in Cummings' mind. He'd been watching Harriet; saw the woman cup her hand to her mouth in delight. The beetle was clinging to the side of the house, a big boy. Sunlight glinted off its glossy shoulders and back.

"*Bienvenido a nuestro pueblo.*" Thought insertion, that's how it felt to Cummings, except he wasn't hallucinating the voice. This insertion was real. The creature had just slipped the sentence into his brain – in *Spanish*. The words translated into something close to "Welcome to our village."

"*Estamos honrados*," Harriet said.

The beetle did three quick up and down moves, its belly clicking lightly against the leafy wall of the long house.

"*Estoy satisfecho por lo que usted Piensa*," another injected thought.

Cummings was still watching Harriet Fine. He believed he and the woman were getting the same messages and that anyone in the immediate area would also get them, exactly the way a person heard spoken words. The beetle's last sentence translated as, "I'm pleased you think so." Cummings wished he had given more attention to his high school Spanish. He saw Harriet's face beam and knew she was getting swept away by it all.

"Are you hearing this," she said, looking at Cummings.

"Creepy but wonderful," he said and smiled back at her.

Harriet looked back at the beetle. "I've got *tons* of questions."

Dark, fast moving clouds blocked the sun. Rain began pecking at the brush and trees. Little storms appeared and disappeared fast in the jungle. The rain was cold. Cummings looked at the sky and wiped his wet face and neck with the flat of his hand. He saw a small flock of gray parrots sailing beneath the clouds.

Harriet just finished asking the beetle if everyone in the community had always lived here or had they gathered together only to heal themselves? Cummings thought this was a good question and the beetle was already answering her. It sounded grateful to at last find someone who showed an interest.

"The cities were very noisy, very violent." These insertions piled one on top of another in Cummings's brain. He'd trouble sorting them out, translating them.

"Are people still killing each other?" the creature was saying to Harriet. It didn't wait for a reply. "I couldn't handle the gangs. One gang killed my eighty-two year old mother, I don't know which one. They soaked her in gasoline and put a match to her. No reason; none that made sense, anyway. People are so angry."

"They're like that everywhere," Harriet said in Spanish.

The beetle still gripped the side of the long house with its narrow hooked claws. It had moved closer to her, to the front of the house. Maybe to get a better look, Cummings guessed. "Go to any city in Venezuela and you can see them yelling in the streets. Fist fights break out, or they grab whatever is available and beat the other person to death – a metal pipe, a trash can lid, a baseball bat. A day doesn't go by without people killing each other. I'm thinking, my Jesus, what will happen, how will I die, what day, what hour."

"With us it's firearms, Harriet said. "We love pistols and automatic weapons."

"I was almost glad when I started growing a shell." The beetle was too involved with its own story to listen to the woman. "My first thought was, they won't be able to hurt me now. I have this shell. I have protection. This is how desperate and anxious I'd become, how insane. People squash bugs. They stomp them to death."

"I didn't know you had such violence," Harriet said.

"We are very modern." The beetle released itself from the wall and landed up right, gray dust raking up about him. "We have our own terrorist groups. Last month one of these groups went into a school house less than twenty kilometers from here and killed many of our children. My twelve-year-old daughter was killed. Can you imagine? Madmen. Who kills children? I almost do not want to change back into myself. I feel safer this way."

RETRACING HERSELF

The Secret Room
Prague, Czech Republic

TWO DAYS BEFORE Lottie had grabbed Franz at the seawall, she'd returned to her brother's house in Prague. Karl's place wasn't a crime scene anymore but she still waited until three-thirty in the morning to break and enter, climbing through the kitchen window that faced the alley. "Don't tell me I don't earn every damn cent I make," whispered that to herself. Lottie had gone into Karl and Judita's bedroom again – talk about a stink. *Jesus.* Blood and bits of brain and skull speckled the headboard and wall. Brown dried blood stained the mattress. No one had bothered to clean up the mess. You'd think they would do that, the police or some type of cleaning service, Lottie thought. She was surprised the police hadn't left the bodies propped upright. "It creeps me out," she said. "Who does this?"

The panel to the rear of the bedroom closet was open and she crouched and entered the small room, waiting until her eyes adjusted to the shadows. Lottie didn't know if it was the police or the kid who'd been there, probably both. But she guessed the kid might have known about the photos and grabbed them before the police, that would've been just like Karl to have a plan. She imagined her brother telling the kid, "If something happens to me, you gotta do such and such." Whatever, run with the pictures; hide them somewhere else. She began searching the secret room. Most of what was there Lottie had seen on her first visit – the same bunch of old black and whites, fat women in old timey bathing suits. Did men really get boners with shit like that? The photos of the women were still in the hidden compartment in the bottom desk drawer. But she couldn't find any of Cummings' pictures, nothing like what he'd shown her, no big-ass insects clinging to the sides of long curved huts in the middle of nowhere.

"And why are these pictures so important?" Lottie had asked him that question the day on the beach at Boca Raton. She was watching the ocean instead of Cummings.

The man waited until she'd turned in her beach chair to look at him. He said, "You've *no* idea?"

"Should I?" Lottie really disliked this bastard.

"Imagine seeing this on one of the cable news channels." Cummings showed her a photo of the village he'd discovered, a large creature attached to the side of a long house. Immediately he took back the picture, his thumb and forefinger snatching it away. He waved the photo at her as he talked. "What do think would happen? Let me tell you *my* scenario. First the C.D.C. calls a 'secret' emergency meeting, thinking they have a new something, a virus. Something. Then some guy with a phone gets video and puts it on a social network. Religious assholes become so excited they take the day off from work. These lunatics *live* for that shit – proves their prophecies, or whatever. Then there's the stock market, skittish on its best day. Now we all sit around watching our already not too good economy tank."

"You think people are that stupid?"

"Yeah. You don't?" Cummings sounded amused.

"Aren't you forgetting the skeptics, the Photoshop crowd?"

"I don't forget anyone." The man had a cold goddamn voice when he wanted to stop a person. "You're willing to take that chance? Wait for the smart ones to grab an *app*? A lot of people love believing the worse. Trust me, people would rather be in the middle of doomsday than be seen as wrong and foolish. 'I knew it, I knew it,' they'd say. 'This is what was foretold, this is the prophecy come true!' Hell, they'd be celebrating."

You couldn't argue with Cummings. And she wasn't convinced he was wrong. In the background of the photograph Cummings had shown her, there were people with bandages on their arms, shoulders and legs – people wounded, or maybe hiding parts of themselves. From the way her employer described the situation, she'd guessed that beneath the bandages were fresh pieces of another creature.

"There are people who say evolution is gradual, it sneaks up on you." Cummings slipped the photograph into the inside jacket pocket of his suit coat. "Others will tell you that we change in a mighty leap, or at least at different speeds."

"I'd say it's happening pretty damn fast."

"Is it? I don't think we know yet." He'd said this in a thoughtful way, as if he had been pondering the physiological shift of things for a while. Lottie hadn't heard that side of him, the non-snotty side, belligerence dipping away and revealing a man who carried a weight that he couldn't, or didn't know, how to share. "I have seen things you wouldn't believe," he said. "For the likes of us, the world is a very big place – lots of little nooks, little shady places that refuse to reveal what we can't imagine seeing."

"Ok, suppose you're right," Lottie said. She and Cummings had moved closer to the water's edge, surf rolling over their bare feet. "What's the world not revealing – according to you?"

"It's like picking out the right shadow," he told her. "You've got to have a notion about your search, don't you think? At the very least you should have your radar going – a suspicious mind."

"How long?" Lottie remembered saying.

He had a bewildered look. "...how long what?"

"I dunno, before the world changes."

"I'm not a fortune teller," he said, a bit indignant.

"I know you don't know ex*act*ly. I get that, okay?" She kept thinking about the photograph he had shown her, all the people in the background of the picture who had bandages wrapped about limbs and torsos. Lottie thought about the people in Prague and the other cities she'd visited in the last year. How many people were bandaged? How many hidden wounds in all the nooks and shady places of the world? She said, "Believe me, I'm very much a person with an open mind. What we're becoming, or what-have-you, that isn't the sort of question I usually consider. But if you were to guess, how long..."

"...before the change takes us all?" Cummings finished her sentence.

"I guess, yes."

"I've no idea," Cummings said. "I wish I did, believe me." Then he added, "But what you saw in the photo was a place of healing. Everyone agreed on that. The people my colleague and I talked to, all of them agreed. They talked about seeing this place in their minds or dreams – a little village in the middle of nowhere. We both heard them say it. This village was where they needed to go."

VISITORS WHO DON'T KNOCK

"... I give his lordship the judge my full and public permission to stop giving secret signs to his paid subordinate down there and give his orders in words instead; let him just say 'Boo now!,' and then the next time 'Clap now!'..."

– The Trial

Max Hoffman's Townhouse
Havana

LOTTIE HAD JUST found Cummings' photographs in a manila envelope under a stack of Franz's Polo shirts. The teakwood bureau was between a small desk and the boy's bed. Franz remained asleep, his breaths steady and even. A wide swatch of Moonlight lay across the foot of his bed and the wood floor. Twenty minutes ago Lottie had climbed onto the balcony of the town house. She'd worked the latch of the double glass doors with her credit card. People should give more attention to security matters, her thinking always, but the obvious shit escapes them.

Now Lottie shut the bedroom door behind her and glanced about the shadowy hall. She felt relief. How tiring she'd become chasing her nephew, *step*-nephew. At least the boy wasn't anything like Karl, you had to give him credit for that. He was probably like the mother, Lottie thought. She had only seen Judita twice but had fallen in love with her gentleness. Why do the nice ones always marry assholes? More than once Lottie had caught herself wishing Judita would take care of her. Let me just crawl into your arms, she'd whispered, right away feeling embarrassed by neediness. Lottie even liked the idea that Judita was a doctor. Imagine having a mother who not only knew what was wrong with you when you got sick but could write a prescription.

Time to get out of here," Lottie thought, bringing herself back to the task.

Night lights near the hall floor made dull yellow circles on the carpet. She'd followed the Cuban woman and the kid to this condo and had waited outside for everyone to get themselves calm. How crazy to grab her nephew in the middle of the street. Jesus, what was she thinking? It showed her how desperate she'd been to finish the job done and get her money.

Less than an hour later, Lottie had watched the boy walk onto the balcony, Max close behind, ushering him inside. She recognized Max right off – the good brother, the one that never teased her. Or didn't tease her all that often, no real meanness in him, always the good guy. She was surprised brother Max didn't have a bigger place. Why would anyone become a professor if the money wasn't good? Of course, this was Cuba and people didn't make money unless they already had money.

Lottie was about to open the glass doors to the balcony when she heard a soft footstep. She turned and saw Max Hoffmann and his pistol. "I have a gun," he said, his voice cobwebbed in sleep.

"Yes, I see."

Max cleared a bit of phlegm from the back of his throat. "Let's be quiet, you and I. No sense waking the boy. Go back to the living room, we'll talk there."

"...and if I don't?"

"You don't, I shoot you."

"You're looking old, Max." Lottie could tell he didn't recognize her. She'd been a skinny thing in those days; had the hair, though – her arms, her legs, that wild tangled crop on her head.

She said, "And your hands are shaking. You nervous, Maxie? I bet what you're doing now is a long way from the classroom. What is it you teach, again?"

Max's eye narrowed, studying her. "...Lottie?"

"Very good," she said. His pistol was aimed at her forehead. A head shot. Amazing, a college professor going for a head shot. "You remembered me, always good to be remembered. What more could a loving sister want from her family? Our brother, Karl the Asshole, he forget me if I went into the next room."

"I'll be damned, it *is* you," Max said. He didn't lower the pistol.

"Can you imagine that jerk?" Lottie said, meaning Karl. She kept talking, hoping to stir a conversation. "When we were kids, the bastard tortured me every five damn minutes. But I just didn't register on his current noteworthy list. Couldn't remember my name, if you can believe that. His own sister and the guy didn't have a clue. He was a self-centered piece of shit."

"Karl had an empathy problem."

"Guess what your brother says to me before I shot him in his fuckin' forehead." And not waiting for a answer, "He says, 'Don't I know you? I can't quite place your face. We know each other, right?' Imagine that, Maxie. Imagine you saying that to your own sis – especially your own sis who's holding a weapon on you. If someone's holding a weapon on me, I'd want them to feel like they're my best friend ever." Lottie shook her head and said, "So I shot him, I had no choice. But I also *wanted* to shoot him, that part's true. I dearly wanted to shoot the son of a bitch. It was like shooting the King of Dicks, who doesn't want to do that?"

"You killed Judita, too." It wasn't a question.

"You can't kill one and not the other," Lottie said. She'd tried to think of every reason *not* to shoot Judita. There was that rule, though. Wives and husbands have a lot of chat time. There are days, weeks and years to fill. After a while it's like talking to a part of yourself. What sealed Judita's fate was her own sweetness. The woman cared enough to match the right face with the right name.

"Lottie? Lottie, dear, is that you?" Judita had said. *Bang.*

Max Hoffmann was asking a question. Lottie must have looked off in her head because Max said, "Hey, are you *listen*ing? You broke into my home. Tell me why I shouldn't call the *policía*, why I shouldn't have you arrested?"

"I took the kid's photos," she said, calm and all business. Her face showed no emotion. That was rule two, never give yourself away – angry feelings, frightened feelings, whatever the feeling, that's kept to yourself. Period. "They belong to my employer. Karl had taken them, no surprise there, right?"

"What photographs? What're you saying?"

"Let's not have a problem." Most of Lottie's jobs went smoothly. No fuss, no muss, she liked to say. Less than a third of her jobs got difficult, and this job had just stepped into that pile. "My employer will get his pictures, I'll get my fee, and all will be right in the world," she said. "Go back to sleep, Maxie, and I'll hop off this balcony, and everybody'll be happy.

Let's not get into the weeds on this one, okay?"

Lottie saw a small shadow behind Max. Franz stepped into the moonlit living room, small and skinny in a summer-t and white jockeys.

"She's got my dad's pictures," the boy said. "He took them from another man, I read it in his diary. Poppa thought he could sell them and get rich. He always had ideas like that."

Lottie decided to go before things got too complicated. As she turned toward the double glass doors, Max fired the Smith & Wesson. The woman grabbed her upper arm and squealed.

She lowered her head, dove through one of the glass doors and jumped the ledge of the narrow balcony.

THE SECOND SESSION

"... truthfully we are not conspiring against you; rather we sit together and we discuss exhaustively with every effort, with jokes, and in earnest, with love, defiance, anger, aversion, resignation, guilt, and with all the strength of our heads and hearts, this dreadful trial in which we and you are entangled..."

— Letter to My Father

Oración a la Milagrosa Polyclinic
Havana, Cuba

FRANZ HAD JUST given a photograph of what he'd started to call "the bug people" to Coro Acosta. It was the one picture he had left thanks to his step-auntie stealing the manila envelope that had the rest of the collection. This picture had been folded down the middle to keep in his wallet. According to his father's diary, Karl Hoffmann had stolen the photos from a man named Cummings.

"I'm guessing you can trust her," his uncle said about the therapist. Franz wanted to talk about the bug people with Acosta. Earlier in the morning the boy and his uncle were sitting in Max's '58 baby-blue Impala convertible in front of the polyclinic. Cuban drivers loved their old cars; Max loved them, too, especially his Impala. Then his uncle said, "Sooner or later we have to trust someone. Otherwise, we've got ourselves a long, lonely life."

The doc seemed okay, the boy thought. She sure

helped him last night. Minutes later Franz was seated across from Coro Acosta in their respective beige plastic chairs – ugly, hard chairs in an ugly room. Nothing felt okay in this room. Even the concrete floor tilted slightly to the right. He wished the doctor had her own private office with peach colored walls and soft chairs and white cotton curtains that billowed in the damp bay breeze.

"Where was the picture taken?" Dr. Acosta said. She'd unfolded the black and white the boy had given her. The psychologist began studying it. She had no particular expression.

"This certainly isn't Cuba."

"My father's diary says Venezuela," the boy said. "—in the jungle. It's not real specific what jungle. He took – *stole* – the pictures from the man who'd gone there."

"You have his diary, too?"

"...yes. But nobody knows." Maybe she'd take the hint. Nobody knew and the boy wanted to keep it that way.

Franz wasn't sure how much he could trust Dr. Acosta, how far he could go with all of it. Until last night he'd even kept the diary a secret from his uncle. Trusting isn't what you do if the parents who loved and protected you suddenly were no more. *Killed.* Learn to say 'killed,' he thought. That's what happened, wasn't it? Killed. *Shot.* Learn to say what happened. Uncle Max told him to say the real words. Franz had felt nervous guarding the photos by himself. He was relieved when the Wolf Lady had taken them. Was it wrong to feel that way? Maybe he should have hid them better. But how could he have known his aunt wanted them? Franz didn't get the value of the things.

Now the doctor looked up from the photograph. "All right," she said. "Maybe we need to talk about confidentiality. Do you know what 'confidentiality' means, Franz?"

"Like a secret?" His best guess.

"Exactly. Like a secret," she said. "What we do here is

a secret – between us, you and me – and I'd only betray our secret if a life was in danger. You understand?"

Franz thought about what Dr. Acosta had just said and nodded. "Okay, yes. I can seeing talking about it to save a life."

After Acosta finished examining the photograph, she gave it back to the boy who folded the picture in half again and put it in his wallet. Then Franz began unbuttoning the left cuff of his white dress shirt, rolling the sleeve up two turns. He removed the gauze about his hand – what had been his hand – he didn't want to think too much about what it was now, what it had become. He needed to keep his confidence.

"I want to show you," Franz said. The last of the bandage dropped away. He expected Dr. Acosta to flinch or turn away but her expression didn't change. She leaned toward him, a curiosity more than anything else. He said, "I used to let my mother clean my hand and fix the new bandage on it. "But since ... you know..." Franz hesitated; looked down at the sunlight and shadows on the slanted concrete floor. "Since she died, I clean it and wrap the bandage myself. I do what she used to do."

"You miss her very much."

"Wouldn't you?"

"...oh yes," Dr. Acosta whispered. "I'd miss her very much, too."

Franz's tears felt hot and his vision blurred. "Yesterday, I said to myself, 'God, I'm an orphan.' Just like that – 'God, I'm an orphan.' I don't know why I hadn't thought about it before – you know, being an orphan – before yesterday, I mean."

"Being alone is a scary thing."

"I don't care that my father died," he said, his voice close to inaudible. "I don't miss him, I don't even feel embarrassed that I don't miss him. Maybe a little embarrassed. I'm not the nicest person in the world, I know that. But I'm supposed to be honest here. Isn't that right?"

Franz didn't want for the doctor to answer. "When you have someone as good as *Matka* – as my mother – everything else doesn't matter – my father drunk, locking me in a closet; the boys at school beating on me because I was small and different, none of it matters."

"You were fortunate to have such a mother," Dr. Acosta said.

"I want to show you," he said, hold up his unbandaged hand. "This is what she helped me with every day. Cleaning the wound, what she called 'my condition,' wrapping it in new bandages. There's nobody now. Do you know what that's like? To have no one who's concerned?'"

"More than you know," Dr. Acosta said.

The boy's hand and wrist were dark-boned and hooked, no fingers, no thumb, all of that had disappeared weeks ago. The sides of the hook were studded with bristles and had the blurry shape of an out of focus darkness. Franz's hand had been sore at the beginning of the change, *very* sore, the way a cracked bone was sore. A few times he'd cried, mostly at night in bed. He didn't want to worry his mother, or have his father think he wasn't a man. This changed part of him was very different than a human hand, another creature entirely. Once Franz imagined that the thing that used to be his hand was an alien from a planet light years away. The alien had spliced itself to the end of his left arm, an emerging being ready to steal the rest of him.

THE COLONY

part 3

"It's got to go," shouted his sister, "that's the only way, Father. You've got to get rid of the idea that that's Gregor. We've only harmed ourselves by believing it for so long..."

— Metamorphosis

Puerto Ayacucho, Venezuela

THEY WERE IN one of the horseshoe-shaped long houses; Harriet Fine, sitting cross-legged beside his bed, what he used as a bed, straw packed into a thick gray cotton casing and stitched together at both ends. Harriet was watching the man as he slept. Outside she could hear voices, villagers gathered about the pop and snap of the campfire. Its orange light reflected on the straw walls about the bed and in between the slow bending of shadows. This afternoon the man had been a beetle on the side of the long house, defying gravity. Now he was finally resting, his narrow, angular face shiny with sweat. His human form not altogether unappealing, Harriet thought.

Several times she'd touched his face for no reason at all. "...Ernesto," she murmured to herself. "Are you really done? Is this the last of it, do you even know?" She wiped his forehead and cheeks with a dry cloth. "How many times can you go through these changes before your body gives up and leaves you stranded or dead?"

A couple of hours earlier he'd screamed twice before releasing his grip and tumbling from the exterior wall of the long house. What were his first words when his transformation was done? "Coming back is like every bone in my body breaking," he'd said in Spanish. Harriet couldn't envision such agony. One summer she had sprained her ankle running in the woods. That was painful enough. Yes, running from some boy – *Harry*, that was his name – the two of them, eleven, twelve, perhaps younger – Harry with the nice teeth who'd asked if he could touch her close-to-nonexistent breasts. She'd wanted to say, Oh, yes. *Please*. Be my guest." But she didn't know how to say that so she ran and giggled and sprained her ankle. God, she had never known that sort of pain. Shocking was what it was.

"Have I been a bother?" Ernesto's first words, his eyes half open. He'd been out since 4:30 in the afternoon. It was now 7:46 in the evening. "Was I an embarrassment?"

"You were very appropriate," Harriet assured him; that, too, in Spanish.

"I didn't tell you how absolutely lovely you are?" He grinned; showed a front tooth outlined in gold.

–A perfect gentleman."

"I'm losing my touch," he said. "Usually, I'm not so perfect."

"Oh, stop."

Ernesto turned from his right side to his back and tried to stretch his muscles and joints. Harriet heard tiny cracks of bone. The man groaned at the self-imposed strain of his limbs and back. "If I don't do this, my joints will lock. If do it, my bones will fracture as I straighten my body. A person can't win for losing."

"How many times have you transformed?"

"This is number fourteen."

Harriet tried picturing herself shuttling from one
form to another, from human to beetle and back again,
the popping of bones, a dietary menu of wood and
dung, the shifting to beetle sight – in the second larval
stage most beetles go temporarily blind as they develop
new, bifocal vision – the trauma of trading one's
complex organism for something alien. Harriet also
realized she'd lead too cloistered a life. Academicians
had a way of side-stepping the dread that tossed
around Ernesto and others like him. Academic stress
was usually without knives and guns and a willingness
to murder for reasons both serious and trite.

"You're ... lovely," Harriet said, feeling an
immediate blush heat her face and neck. "Oh I'm *so*
sorry. I didn't mean – the day has been exhausting,
Ernesto. I've never seen anything like it. The way
people here struggle. The way *you* struggle. It's
heartbreaking. Please, forgive my ... my enthusiasm.
I'm worn from the day."

"–Not to worry, señora."

"–Harriet."

"All right, Harriet then."

"Normally I'm not the type who'd say an unladylike
thing." Her angst refused to let go. "I-I don't do that.
But who'd ever believe your life, what you go through,
what everyone here goes through – it's remarkable."

"You are the first woman who's ever called me
lovely." Ernesto said. He placed his palm atop her
hand. She let it stay. He said, "You shouldn't be
embarrassed, Señora Harriet. I don't mind being
lovely."

"I'm not embarrassed. Well a little embarrassed."

"You are lovely too."

"I'm fat," Harriet said.

"This is a good thing, yes? To have more?"

Harriet Fine was about to tell Ernesto, no, it wasn't a

good thing at all, not for beauty, not for health, but she'd heard firearms and smelled burning oil or gasoline. The villagers just outside the long house were screaming. Elijah Cummings was with the others. He'd wanted to sit by the campfire in the community area and talk to the ones who were done with their transitions and the ones who were still caught with between flesh and shell. Harriet had started to see the fire through the window above Ernesto's bed. Two of the long houses closer to the jungle were in flames. Smoke from the other dwellings hovered inside their own house; clung to the edge of the windows. Ernesto had started coughing.

"Their cure will be here before we know it," Cummings had told Harriet earlier in the afternoon. "We don't want these people thinking it's the village. 'Getting away from it all' has never been a cure. That's a vacation. The cure is in always pharmaceuticals. The cure is in science, Dr. Fine, not peace of mind."

THE WAYS
SCHOOL CAN
SUCK

"As soon as her eyes met K's it seemed to him that her look decided something concerning himself, something which he had not known to exist, but which her look assured him did exist."

– The Castle

UNCLE MAX WAS giving Franz the run down on middle schools in Havana; he did it on his nephew's first day, several weeks ago now, and he was doing it again this morning. "Both schools and health are subsidized 100 % by the government," his uncle said. They were sitting in Max's Impala at 6:54 AM, parked near Franz's school. The boy felt he was always sitting in the car for something or other. Franz would be glad when he no longer needed chauffeuring around. Classes began at 7 AM exactly and ended at 7PM. The academic year was longer, too – September to July. Franz didn't like Cuban schools. They worked too long and the work was hard. Teachers liked telling Franz and his classmates how former students out-performed neighboring countries and how everyone had an obligation to do good work and continue this tradition.

"Some boys want to beat me up," Franz said to his uncle.

"Why would they do such a thing?"

"Look at me. I'm different." The boy was staring at the silver nylon book bag on his lap. "I'm European, for one thing, and I'm a Jew. I'm also pale, a lot paler than most of them. *And* I don't like baseball. That's a big one, believe me. I've never understood the rooting-for-your-team stuff. Then yesterday our teacher, Mrs. Duarte, said I was 'a fine addition to her class.' Right in front of everybody. 'Franz always raises his hand,' she'd said. He always knows the answers, too. Everyone should take a lesson from Franz.' Can you imagine?"

"Oh, boy. She doesn't have a clue," Uncle Max said.

"All the guys turned around and looked at me – girls, too, but mostly guys." Franz could hear the anxiousness in his voice and he took a breath and tried to calm himself. He said, "It's like that mafia movie. You know, when Michael kisses Fredo on the mouth and says, 'You broke my heart.' It's like that – the kiss of death. What did I ever do to her?"

"Why not have a talk with your teacher?"

"And say what?" Occasionally Franz didn't understand his uncle.

There were people who only knew how to dig a hole deeper. Mrs. Duarte was one of those people. She came into the world Shovel Ready. He imagined having a talk with this woman only to have her immediately turn to the class and say, "Instead of hating this very nice boy, all of you should admire Franz. Learn from him. Notice how he always calls me ma'am, for example. Yes, ma'am, no ma'am. This is how all of you should treat your elders. He's a breath of fresh air, if you ask me." There were teachers you trusted and teachers you didn't trust – mostly, you didn't trust them. Mrs. Duarte wasn't an evil person, but evil and naiveté do equal damage. Franz imagined her telling him, "Am I supposed to know how my words will be taken? "Yes, you *are* supposed to know, he thought. You're there to teach me and protect me. Being stupid isn't an excuse. Not paying attention isn't an excuse. What's wrong with you? Who told you ignorance is forgivable? I *never* okayed that? How many students have gotten themselves beat up because of you?"

"Things all right, Franz?" His uncle looked concerned.

"One of the guys calls me 'Mr. Perfect.' Usually he says it in front of his friends." Franz had made a fist with his right hand and was kneading the soft nylon book bag on his lap. This guy – Luis is his name – he's going to fight me. I don't know when, exactly. But he's gonna do it, Uncle, probably the day he gets a big enough audience."

"You can't be sure of that," Max said, his hand on his nephew's shoulder.

"I don't have to be Mr. Perfect to know what's going on," Franz glanced out the car window on the passenger's side. Max had parked the blue Impala in front of the school. The boy watched his classmates and others climb the concrete steps toward the front door of *École Secondaire Benitez-Turbiano.* Franz said, "Luis is not too smart, but he's taller than me. And fat – he likes bumping kids with his stomach. People laugh when he does that. I can see how much he likes to make people laugh, particularly the popular girls. Boys, too – the one who are good at sports."

"Do you know how to fight?"

"My father taught me," Franz said. Fighting lessons with Karl Hoffmann was another way the man could knock him around. Franz got very good at ducking and dodging. He could throw a good punch, too. Once he knocked his father down. Karl's anger flickered across his eyes the way clouds travel under the sun. Franz said, "Poppa always scared me a little. I never knew what he'd do next."

"Karl was a good fighter," Max said, maybe thinking about a beating of his own, bullies bully everyone. "Personally, I prefer talking things out. But brother wasn't big on patience. I can recall the times I told him to calm down and think a problem through. Must have done that at least twice a week."

"I know how to move my feet," Franz said.

His uncle studied the boy's face. "Have you ever fought?"

"Well not an actual fight, no."

"...never?"

Franz knew this wasn't the answer Max cared to hear. He wanted to reassure his uncle. There was nothing to worry about, that's what he would've liked to say. But the boy didn't know what might happen. He imagined Fatso Luis shoving him down on the cafeteria's concrete floor – worse, the guy bouncing on his chest, all two hundred and fifty pounds of him. Franz imagined hearing his ribs snap. And when would *that* happen, what week, what day, what hour? Because it *was* going to happen and probably sooner than later. Nothing like munching down on a nice Salisbury steak and some fried bananas while cheering on two pissed off guys beating the shit out of each other.

I should get my butt knocked around, Franz thought. A few good hard smacks for not being there when my parents needed me. Dr. Acosta had called that one survivor's guilt. Franz didn't much care what she called it. What did she know, anyway? They weren't her parents.

THE BANDAGED

"Come and 'ave a look at this, it's dead, just lying there, stoned dead."

– Metamorphosis

San Francisco de Paula
70 km. Outside Havana

ARIA MALOOF LOOKED at the back of the photograph she'd found in Lottie's dresser drawer under her panties and bras. The photo had been in a manila envelope with lots of others like that one. On the back of the picture, it said:
Property of Elijah C. Cummings
The Colony
On the Padamo River
Venezuela
The people in the photo reminded her of the dead insects Lottie had pinned under glass and hung on the wall. They had iridescent shells, long, black twiggy legs, hooks with points. They had the details of insects. But some were different than that. Human faces shown through black bristles and squatty necks. There was an infrequent yet recognizable arm, legs that could support and lift a torso. Many bandaged, too. What Aria noticed most wore bandages, strips of dirty cloth unraveling about a limb, a neck and jaw. Clean white cotton bandages were rare but very noticeable.

"Why is everyone so wounded?" Aria had recently said to Lottie; this a week ago before she'd seen the pictures. "It's like the world has become accident prone. Have you noticed – here in town, the city? What's happening to people? I see it on TV, too."

"I've no idea what you mean," Lottie said. But it sounded like she absolutely knew what I meant, Aria thought. Then Lottie said, "Don't go making something out of nothing. You're famous for doing that type of shit. Like the couple of times I had to go back to Prague, a stranger listening to you would've figured I was part of a great worldwide conspiracy."

They were sitting under an awning on their front porch and drinking cold vodka in small round glasses. Lottie had also brought out some chilled, glazed figs. "I still think that," Aria said. She didn't want to confront Lottie about the dead step brother and the sister-in-law, what she'd seen in one of the online Prague newspapers. That was for another time. The photograph concerned her. Too many people were walking around patched in gauze and adhesive tape, too many with canes and crutches.

"You think I'm part of a conspiracy, Aria?"

"Well something's going on."

Lottie did a dramatic eye roll. "Listen to yourself."

"Do you *ever* pay attention?" Aria watched the afternoon heat zigzagging up slowly from the dirt road in front of their home. "You know, do you look at the TV news, things in our everyday lives? The walking wounded, I call them."

"Perhaps I'm too self involved," Lottie said, changing the subject. Did she *want* the conversation to go into an uncomfortable place and get derailed? That's what Aria guessed. Lottie was saying, "Isn't that what you tell me – how self-absorbed I am? What am I supposed to be seeing? Explain it again. What signs of doom?"

"I'm sure it's my imagination." Aria finished her vodka and took the bottle from the white Styrofoam ice chest on the whicker table between them and poured herself another drink. "I see lots of banged up people – arms, legs, what-have-you."

"Yeah. I see that, too, actually."

"And what do you think about it?" Aria wanted to know; amazed that Lottie answered so honestly. This was the question of the day as far as Aria was concerned, "What do you think?" I need another option, another set of eyes, she'd thought. Then she'd said, "Am I going crazy? Are people falling apart?"

"Who knows, hon. The world is a dangerous place."

Not exactly a candid option. "Yeah, the world's dangerous," Aria said. "But this is *different* than that. See, I think people have become more *aware* of danger. Hell, the danger may even be *less* than it was, say a hundred years ago. It's really not about the danger, *per se*, it's how we think about danger, the way we *learn* about it. God, it may be our instincts, you know. I mean our thinking could still be at the shallow end of the gene pool, but our *sense* about danger has improved."

"You really have been thinking about this," Lottie said. She'd been looking down at her vodka, rolling the small cold shot glass between her thumb and forefinger. "Let it go, darling. Don't get yourself stirred up – not that I'm disagreeing with you." Lottie had put the palm of her hand on Aria's bare, tan arm. Aria remembered the feel of it, the warmth of Lottie's fingers. "I haven't thought much about it, but I do see your point. Eventually the dumb asses among us might get a better sense of things. Why the fuck not? I just don't want you to worry."

Aria Maloof let go of remembering their conversation. She focused on the photograph again, one of many such pictures she'd found in the bedroom dresser. What would a person call them, the individuals in the photo – insect people? Aria didn't know. She'd tried looking at their illness like, well, leprosy, maybe, but that would be a disease, wouldn't it?

Aria sat on the edge of the queen sized bed and began removing the Reebok and the white ankle length sock off her left foot. Didn't diseases have to do with bacteria or viruses? She felt perfectly normal, really – no fever, no pain or upset stomach, or whatever. She crossed her legs, left ankle on right knee, looking down at her foot. The left foot seemed darker than the right one; skinnier, too.

FARR
PHARMACEUTICALS

"... Sometimes it's impossible to understand what the judge thinks he's doing..."

−The Trial

Company Headquarters
Philadelphia

"THEY'LL BELIEVE IT'S slash and burn," Breton Farr said. He was standing behind his desk, his back to Elijah Cummings, staring out the glass that covered the back wall of his office. The man was early fifties, rimless glasses, hair a black and gray buzz cut. He wore a tailored suit with a white starched shirt and a nondescript tie. The glass wall was tinted a soft gold color and the office had a perpetual sunset look. Mr. Farr said, "Locals set fire to their jungles all the time. It's how they farm. We'll plow it over; plant corn or something. Soybeans. They love soybeans. The natives will see it as a gift. 'From Our family to Your Family,' isn't that what we say?"

"People were killed," Cummings said, his voice close to inaudible. He hated Farr's office, chrome and black leather furniture, three white lacquered walls empty of pictures. The bleached pine floors were polished but had no rugs. Minimalist shit, Cummings thought. Like it's owner.

Then he said, "You can't just go into a place and burn everything."

"I have shareholders." Mr. Farr turned, his grin big enough to show perfectly capped teeth, or maybe his teeth were the real deal. Who was Cummings to devalue a person's teeth? Last year Farr lost his wife, Taylor, to breast cancer. Elijah had attended the funeral; wanted to do it. Hell, sent the man a sympathy card, for Christ-sake. Terrible experience losing a loved one. But at this moment, Cummings wanted to take back the card. Breton Farr was saying, "I'm judged on my decisions, sport. My job depends on keeping those darling shits rich and happy. Here's the bottom line: pharmaceuticals isn't a game for pussies. You feel me?"

Feel me? Cummings thought. Unbelievable. Who's this guy – some old Episcopalian rapper? Feel me. Five or six months after Taylor's death, Farr had started going out with a 36 year old Dominican divorcée, Paloma. She had a thirteen year old kid, Jabes, who looked at Breton Farr as if he was the devil. This new family had changed Farr's vocabulary into a mix of Dominican Spanish and Yale. And with all of that, Cummings bet even Jabes didn't say "feel me." That crap had officially become what middle-aged white men said to one another. It had to do with the loss of their hair and the lag of their cocks.

"Pharmaceuticals don't cure the sick," Farr said. He was looking out the glass wall for the second time, the sprawl of Center City Philly. City Hall was less than two blocks away, and Farr's office was eye level with the statue of William Penn. "Curing the sick doesn't make us rich, Elijah. Do you know what makes us rich?"

Breton Farr could also be a condescending prick. Cummings had worked for the company going on twenty-three years – so, yes, he knew what made them rich. He'd heard this before, *many* times before, but the boss is the boss and the boss can say whatever he wants as many times as he wants. Farr said, "–Keeping people just sick *enough*."

Right in that Goldilocks zone, Cummings thought.

"Right in that Goldilocks zone," Farr murmured, his eyes fixed on the face and tricorn hat of William Penn. "That's where fortunes are made, old friend. Am I right?" Cummings thought no answer was necessary. Farr said, "That's what got you and me very rich."

That's also what lost Elijah Cummings his wife and their twins –girls, two lovely girls. Sixty hour work weeks; more, if needed: late nights, weekends, and on the road more than he would've liked.

What do you say?

Some people understood business and what it took to run a business, and some people lived in another universe on another planet, the planet where elves and fairies brought you vodka and did your nails.

"You have no conscience," Bethany Ann liked to tell him. Bethany knew the agenda, the corporate routine. A company invented "maintenance" drugs to insure a patient's continued good health. A company didn't make money with cures. The pharmaceutical industry was a subscription industry like any drug trade, legal or illegal. Like magazines and newspapers, like the fruit of the month club. Cures were never the best bottom line for share holders," she'd said that, many times. "Be honest, darling, you sell the 'possibility' of a cure."

"–My wife Gandhi."

"Go on, make jokes."

Bethany was slim then, a bunch of very sexy bones. And Elijah was about 80 pounds lighter. Her skin stayed tan year round, too – tanning beds, predominately, including the MRI lookalike he'd bought for her 33rd birthday. I should've just set fire to my money, he thought. Would a person invest in a stock that had a 50-50 chance of success? That's what marriage is, isn't it, a statistically bad investment? Young people marry for beauty and don't pay attention to the other 90 percent until the sex stops and the everyday becomes either silence or arguments. Nothing was worse than married lonely.

Cummings didn't miss Bethany Ann at all. But he did miss the twins, Patsy and Paula. His ex wanted to have *three* children with their first names beginning in "P." "That'd be terrific, Eli," she'd said. "We'd call them 'our three Ps in a pod.' Don't you think that's adorable? Seriously."

How does a person have wild financial success and keep his values and his family? How does that work, considering the requirements, the piano and the clarinet recitals, the birthdays, the cookouts, the supervised sleepovers, soccer game attendances and practices, special times with one child then the other – so everybody would feel "special" – children aren't to be taken lightly.

Exs can always remarry and go about their businesses. Bethany Ann did that, more power to her. Kids, though, they aren't that lucky. Kids can't wipe away their fathers, the biological ones, the originals. They can't say, Ed or Joe is my daddy now, my *new* daddy. Your flesh and blood knows that's bullshit, every kid in the universe knows that. Yet mommies always seem to bad mouth daddies, don't they? They can't resist it. Talk about your post-marital propaganda. "Let me tell you, Patsy and Paula," his ex had reportedly said, according to the twins: "Your so-called father is an emotionally crippled individual, okay? People require more than *things*. You can't buy people off with *things*. You girls will realize that later in your life."

The twins loved him; still loved him. Their Mother's kryptonite hadn't weakened that love.

Cummings had started sending his daughters cards and pictures from all over the world when they were very young and he'd never stopped doing that. He always told them how much he loved them and how proud he was of what they were doing with their lives. Last week Elijah even told them about his friend Harriet Fine, the biologist from Florida, who died in a fire in the Venezuela jungle and how bad that had hurt him, how terrible he felt. Cummings couldn't sleep or eat since the tragedy happened, but he assured Patsy and Paula that life's ups and downs wouldn't get the best of him.

Of course, they were much older now and understood what men say to themselves.

BAÑO DE
LOS CHICOS

"I thought I had injured you (not me) through this, and I felt guilty – as I always did, for I was guilty through and through."

— Letter to My Father

École Secondaire Benitez-Turbiano
Havana

THERE WERE SIX boys waiting for Franz and the fat boy bully Luis Meza. Franz had been pushed into the bathroom by Luis, and now was quickly·sizing up friends and foes – okay not friends, exactly, but kids who were anxious enough to sympathize with his situation, kids who'd maybe help stop the beating. He didn't see anyone like that. Two girls had also slipped into the boy's bathroom. Franz knew them by name only, two classmates. Both Ana and Ibbie liked watching a good fight. They also liked fighting; liked going headlong into the thick of anything. Both girls were tall for their ages and wore sleeveless blouses so other kids could see their muscles and wouldn't fuck with them. The one called Ibbie had a black patch over her right eye. Franz thought the girls were more like squadmates with common interests instead of friends.

"I'm gonna tear your ass up, Chico." Luis said that in English.

"You don't even know me."

"I know you're ugly." Luis laughed and glanced at the others to see how he was doing. A couple of the boys were smiling. The girls looked bored. They were leaning more on one leg than the other, hips extended sideways, arms crossed.

Fat boy Luis walked around Franz, a tight circle, his fists up and blocking his face. The boy's fists were close to his face. Franz was turning as the fat boy turned, always staring at his eyes. Both his fists were raised, too, his left hand wrapped in fresh white gauze.

Franz thought about what his father had taught him.

"You know how people say don't kick a man when he's down?" Karl Hoffmann had said that to him when they were sitting on a park bench in the town square across from their house. The afternoon was bright and crisp and the leaves were mostly red and yellow and they'd float off the trees, leaf after leaf. "God, doesn't that make you want to vomit? Have you heard that 'don't hit a man when he's down' expression?"

"Yes, Poppa."

"Well it's bullshit, okay? It's little queer boy talk. Right off you got to hit the guy in the face. You hit him in the face two, three times, if you can, if you're lucky enough. Hell, hit him four times. Aim for the nose and teeth. After that, kick his balls. And you do that until you see blood. Understand? You're not asking this bitch on a date. You don't want to kiss him. You want him to stay *down*. Got it?"

"Yes, poppa."

"Okay, good. If you don't see blood, you're not doing it right."

Franz stopped thinking about his father and focused on Luis. Every so often Franz glanced at the six boys and two girls in the school bathroom. The floor was white tiles, urinals on the left, stalls on the right, all of it going the length of the room. Large overhead windows let in the late morning sun and the light reflected off the tile floor, the glare hiding their expressions.

Luis jabbed at Franz twice, nice quick ones, a move his father would've liked. Franz leaned back each time and avoided both of them. His father would've like that, too.

"You afraid to take a swing?" Luis said. He looked at his audience and gave a grin but Franz didn't see anyone grinning back or hear anyone. To be fair, the sun *was* bright. Maybe he had a kid or two on his side. He'd have at least one or two, Franz thought. Then Luis said, "Hit me, *maricon*. C'mon, be a man, don't shame your family." The boy lowered his fists and stuck out his chin. "Right here, c'mon. I'll give you a free shot."

"I don't need a free shot."

"I'll give you ten seconds." Luis looked at the small group of classmates."Count with me," he said to the kids. "C'mon, one ... two ... three..." Nobody was counting but the fat boy. Again Luis said, "Hey, let's count it down together. Show the new guy we give people a chance."

You're not dating the bitch, Franz heard his father say.

A cloud drifted across the sky outside the bathroom window, dulling the sunlight, bringing a shadow. A boy behind two other boys had his arm resting in a beige cloth sling.

Franz swiped at Luis. The swing connected just below the right eye, a hard punch that sent his opponent to the concrete floor, ass first. Luis made an *oufff!* sound. Franz grabbed his own fist, the bandaged left hand, his body immediately bending at the waist.

"Shit, *shit*," he muttered. "I can't believe I did that."

The pain was a brutal, flashing shock from his fist to his head. Franz thought he was going to faint and willed himself to keep standing. For ten or fifteen seconds his knees felt like they were made of air. The white gauze bandage had become undone. He watched it fall toward the tile floor. Now his bristled, hook was exposed, what used to be his hand. Everyone was staring at it, the six boys; Ana and Ibbie, too. None of them said anything. No hoots or jeers, no laughter. They stayed quiet. Franz wished he could disappear. He imagined himself collapsing into ashes, a magical wind rush him out the bathroom window.

"Damn, are you guys *seeing* this shit," Luis said, holding the side of his face where he'd been punched, and he nodded toward Franz's left hand, that misshapen bony darkness. "Look at *that* – that ... that *thing* – how is that fair? I got to fight some freak? Where is the even playing field? Am I right?"

Ibbie had just removed her eye patch. The tall girl's right eye was a swollen, iridescent honeycomb. A fly's eye, a beetle, Franz didn't know. The shadows in the bathroom were gone now and the window let in the sunlight. It sparkled the tiny crevices of the honeycomb. The boy in the back tossed aside his cloth sling and his blue long sleeved shirt. Black bristles cover him, hand to bicep. Others began stripping away clothing. The beginning of shells appeared on their shoulders, their backs, the rise of their necks. Franz watched Luis slump, his chest becoming concave, the bloom of defeat and fear, the two feelings melting together in a weird, bittersweet acceptance.

"I'm doing this for you guys," he whispered.

The six boys and two girls descended on Luis. Franz could hear them chattering.

CONFESSION
part 2

"Despite what you say I have not lost my family sense, on the contrary it endures, but as a negative sense which spurs my (naturally, never ending) inner flight from you."

— Letter to My Father

Iglesia de San Francisco de Paula
San Francisco de Paula

"I'M NOT A religious person," Aria Maloof said.

Farther Jorge didn't answer.

"I have no desire to *become* religious," Aria said. She was inside the confessional. Twigs of yellow light mingled with shadows. The cubical also had its own embedded smells – Jorge's cinnamon aftershave and traces of many a quick smoke. She said, "Another thing, please don't think I'm some black sheep who needs saving, or whatever you guys think. Religion has always seemed odd to me. If we didn't think the way we do – about dying and our little tragedies – we probably wouldn't need religion. But people are always dying, and tragedies are everywhere. That'll happen to me, too – dying, I mean. I get it."

"When was your last confession, child?"

"Two weeks, I think. Maybe less."

"You don't want this becoming a habit." An observation.

"Let's get something straight, Father – you know,

131

clear the air." Aria wasn't thrilled with tiny dark rooms, either. Just a coffee and a chat at the cafe would've been fine. The one in town had outdoor tables. Maybe at some point she'd asked him, not that Aria wanted to have a regular thing and get all chummy. "I could go to one of the clinics in Havana and wait six hours and see a therapist," she said. "Probably get in a fight while I'm waiting, or have to listen to some poor *mamacita* tell me about her grandchild the drug addict. But I decided to come here. I don't know why, the lines are shorter."

"And the company?"

"I like it that you grab a smoke between the bullshit."

"It's very difficult to get away," Father Jorge said. Aria thought he sounded embarrassed, or perhaps apologetic. "I'm not without my sins. Along with the occasional cigarette, I like a nice imported beer. Not everyday, mind you. But, well, from time to time. We priests aren't that much different from anyone else, really."

There was something creepy about telling her he was a regular guy, that he drank and smoked. Priest *aren't* regular guys, she thought. They didn't fuck and they didn't get Casual Fridays. Special guys didn't do ordinary things. But she bet there wasn't one of them who hadn't longed for a regular life, she was sure of it. Didn't they want to flirt and get drunk with *some*body? Wasn't the world still a lonely place?

Aria was determined to tell him what had been troubling her. Who else did she have, really? She needed to talk to Lottie but was it the right thing to do and how did a person do it in a tactful way? And Lottie felt too deeply about disturbances in their relationship. Her partner liked acting tough but she was far too sensitive. Aria took a quiet breath and said, "I've become ill, father. I'm afraid to tell anyone, even a doctor – especially a doctor. I'm afraid the people in charge would put me away somewhere. I know that sounds paranoid. What's the old saying? 'Just because you're paranoid, doesn't mean people aren't after you?' That's how I feel. If I open my mouth to the wrong person, I'm gone forever."

"Nothing's that bad," Father Jorge said, a "there, there" manner to his voice. Aria wondered if it had been a good idea to confide in him at all. Most religious people were people of extremes – the world was either coming to an end or God was making the blind see and the deaf hear – no sense of balance, no sense of reason. But what could you expect when faith was built on an End of Days catastrophe? Every hint of it brought a little orgasm and a little terror. Father Jorge said, "I'm guessing your balance is gone. Our imaginations do get the better of us."

"Is that what you think?" Shit, the guy was a hoot.

"I can't tell you the times I thought the modern world was beyond redemption," the priest said. "My imagination taunted me. Then I'd read about, say, the horrors of the inquisition, or the violence of the crusades, or the painful deaths women endured – the Salam trials, that business. Religion collects the cruel, I'm not oblivious to that."

"You surprise me, Father."

"The priest paused. Aria could see the shadow of his profile through the wood slats separating them. He said, "We're not perfect. Parts of the world are still primitive, but I get hopeful. Maybe I'm foolish, but we've come so very far."

Aria slipped the photo she'd taken from Lottie's bureau through a slat in the confessional window. She felt Father Jorge take it from her. Aria said, "I'm sick like that, like you see in the picture. Have you ever seen or heard about this type of sickness?"

"...oh God," the priest whispered.

"I take that as a no?"

Where ... where did you get this?" He wanted to know.

"Answer my question."

"Are these people? What are they?"

"Would you consider that a medical condition," Aria said. She was looking through the window slats, squinting, trying to see his reaction through the shadows. He held the photo with one hand, his fingers trembling. She said, "Could it be a virus? I'd like to think there was a medical explanation."

"You must ask a doctor," Farther Jorge said, his voice raspy. I-I'm not a doctor. You should see Estefan Cruz at the *Hospital Popular*. The doctor is a friend. He may know of this thing."

"–But in *your* opinion."

The priest took an audible breath, released it slowly. His voice was soft, hesitant. "What am I supposed to tell you? Not all things can be explained. Obviously this isn't like the flu or a broken leg. These poor creatures," he murmured. "This is why we turn to God, Ms. Maloof. God is here for events we don't understand, for mysteries we can't so easily dismiss."

THINKING BIG

"Tell me, now, in what way do I hide anything from you?"

– The Castle

Miami International Airport
Miami, Florida

LOTTIE WAS SITTING in a booth at the Palm Bar near Gate G4. Miami International had a long glass wall on the other side of the walkway and sunlight flooded the waiting areas and her booth with bright afternoon light. She arrived seven minutes ago and was already working on a chilled, slightly watered down tumbler of vodka. Her plan was to have a couple of drinks then rent a Lincoln or one of those big ass Buick's – preferably a black one – and drive the 26 miles to Boca Raton to see Elijah Cummings and get her money.

She downed the first vodka and ordered the second. Her drinking arms was throbbing, the spot where her brother had shot her; grazed her, really. The doc had given Lottie scripts for antibiotics and Percocet. She'd gotten the antibiotics but tossed the Percocet. She didn't trust herself with that shit. Ibuprofen would be just fine, thanks. Lottie took her cell from the side pocket of her leather handbag and dialed Cummings' number.

"Yeah?"

"That's how you answer a phone?"

"Lottie darling," Cummings said, immediately cheering up. "How's the girl?" He didn't wait for an answer. "I've got a bag of money here with your name on it."

"And a secure phone, I hope."

"Always."

All right, she thought, that was probably true. "I've got your pictures. Those are some fucked up folks."

"What can I say? The world's a fascinating place."

"No argument," she said.

"This is why we get along. Two professionals."

The waiter brought Lottie's second vodka. He was one of those Miami hipsters, skinny jeans, a 5 o'clock shadow going on 7. His name tag read "Taylor." Perched back on a perfect 100 dollar hair cut was one of those straw hats with the little brim. Lottie wanted to shoot Taylor in his special place. She cupped the phone and whispered to the waiter, "Nice hat."

"It's a Stetson straw," Taylor whispered back.

"You know, I had a feeling." Did he blush? Lottie thought he did. As he walked away, she said into her cell, "Hipsters. The world is become entirely too precious."

"You brought the merchandize with you?" Ah, down to business.

"Why would I come here empty-handed?" Lottie said. She had only two of his photos in a manila envelope; along with that, she'd taken 120 photos of her middle finger. In color. Lottie also had a Beretta 92A1 with a silencer.

"Let's use the same spot," Cummings said. "–That beach where we first met, do you remember? Very secluded, very good for business?"

"How could I forget, Elijah, dear." A little flirty.

Over the months Lottie had learned to hate this fat bastard. What the world came down to was respect, she thought. You respect me and I'll respect you. Two adults that didn't take the world personally, what could be simpler, what could be wiser? All too often wounded egos got in the way. God only knows when these wounds occurred. Babies fighting over too little titty milk – or worse, babies drowning in far too *much* milk – who knew how the ball got rolling.

These Baby Battles played themselves out again and again. Hurt feelings raged against all comers, law suits for some, drive-byes for others. There were plots to humiliate the ever-changing parade of enemies, plots that left foes with nothing but a beggar's life.

"What will you do with all that money?"

"Pay off my student loans," Lottie said. All what money? she thought. Seventy-five grand got her food stamps.

"I never know if you're serious," he said.

"Oh you'll know. Do you have my bank number?"

"I do," Cummings said. "I've already wired the money. Call it an act of good faith. Check your phone."

Lottie had a sip of her vodka and began looking through her emails. The second vodka was still icy enough to sting on the way down. Her shoulders, neck and chest felt warm and soothed. It melted the hard edges of the world. Isn't that's what Aria liked to say? Lottie loved Aria; had loved her for years. More than that, really, Lottie confided in her, trusted her. How often does a person find that?

"I know what you do," Aria had told her. She'd said it more than once. The last time was on their front porch as they watched a hot gust whirl sand across the road. Aria had said, "Will you ever stop? How can you be so loving to me and do the things you do?"

...my last time, Lottie thought. I'm getting too old for this type of shit, anyway. One final, glorious moment, that's all she needed. To see the rage on Elijah Cummings' face as he shuffled through one color photo of her middle finger after another. Then Lottie would shoot him. Then she'd take her money and leave. Lottie imagined a week passing, maybe two before she walked into Farr Pharmaceuticals and named her price.

What did she think the photographs were worth to the company? She had no idea, but here was the real question: what was it worth to the pharma boys to keep a potentially *free* cure a secret? Ah, *there* it was, the email. It had been sent a half hour ago to her bank in the BVI. Seventy-five thousand USD. The wonders of technology, she thought.

ON THE BACK STEPS AFTER SCHOOL

"From the start you were against anything that interested me, and especially the manner of my enthusiasm; and here it was the same."
                                    – Letter to My Father

École Secondaire Benitez-Turbiano
Havana

THE TALL GIRL with the patch over her right eye had her own pictures. These were all kids close to her age, some Franz had seen in different classes and on the streets. Ibbie Reyes and Franz sat on the concrete steps in the back of the school. The early afternoon was already hot and the sky had no clouds. Franz figured he was a year younger than the girl. Ibbie reminded him of a beautiful pirate. Her legs were slim and tan and her black hair was pulled back and held together with turquoise clips. This was a 90 minute recess and kids were eating their lunches or playing sports – baseball, soccer, mostly – while others huddled in small groups, talking loud and laughing. Somewhere a radio was broadcasting music. Ibbie said the song was an old one by Juan de Marcos Gonzalez.

"Where did you get them?" Franz said, nodding at her photos she'd taken from her handbag to show him.

"I have a camera."

Franz could tell the girl liked him but was annoyed at his question and he didn't want to mess everything up. When Ibbie told him she had a camera, the girl sounded insulted. As if to say, do you think I'm so poor I don't have a camera?

"You are very fortunate," Franz said. He wanted his new friend to feel okay again. "I wish I had a camera. I'd take pictures everyday. A person can stop a piece of life with a camera. When the years pass, you can look at your pictures and see all the people and things you've forgotten."

"It's an old one. My auntie had it for years." Ibbie had stuffed the pictures back into her handbag. Now she was swaying her shoulders to the music from the radio, her thumb and middle finger posed, ready to snap to the rhythm. If she'd been upset, Franz couldn't tell that now. Her tone was friendly. "I don't ever use it," Ibbie said. "You know, the camera. I'd felt bad about my eye, how I was different than people. Then my friends started showing me what was wrong with them – an arm, a shoulder, a part of their legs. You know, the dark bones with the bristles. The bits of shell, too. They said I shouldn't feel bad. So I started taking pictures of them, not their faces or anything, ,just the places where they were changing. I'd look at them when I'd get depressed."

"I thought I was alone, too." Franz said. He looked down at the concrete steps and smiled.

"I should thank Luis, I'm glad we had that fight; glad you guys showed up. Usually you don't meet a lot of people in the bathroom. Or anywhere, really."

Ibbie was still moving to the music. She nudged him and giggled, never missing a beat. "People care about you, Franz. You're very likeable, very sincere."

"Does that include you?" He felt his cheeks go hot.

Ibbie quit the music and looked at Franz. "I like you, okay," the girl said. Then she looked at the kids in the school yard and said, "You're too sensitive and too pale. European boys are that way; Americans, too. When fat Luis fell, you should have cut off a piece of ear like they do with the bulls. We have different rules here. You should've taken some blood. It's the way you stop a Cuban boy."

"I'm not like that," Franz said.

"Maybe you should learn."

"My father would've liked you," Franz said. His father always worried that Franz wasn't tough enough to weather dangers, that life would defeat him. His mother didn't worry about him in that way. 'Just find out how to live your own life,' she'd say. Then Franz told Ibbie, "My father believed boys had to be tough to get respect. 'Tough boys get the beautiful girls,' he would say. 'You see it in nature.' This is what he would tell me. 'Look at how the best females mate with the strong ones. They know who will protect the family, who can do the job.' I never felt I was that boy, the one who could win the beautiful girl. I always thought beautiful girls expected too much. Such a girl wasn't worth the aggravation."

"But you're the guy who shows up," Ibbie said. "– To fight Luis, for example. That's like ninety percent, *querido*. Men, they show up. Showing up is everything. That says much about your heart, your *valor*. You also knocked Luis on his ass. This is very good, I wanted to cheer. But then you walk away. You're like the bullfighter who has no stomach for blood," she said. "They walk away like they are *humanitario*. But Cubans know the truth. Bullfighters who walk away are *debiles* – how do you say?"

"Weak. No, you mean coward."

"Si, these bullfighters fool themselves," Ibbie said.

"But I can teach you. I'm very good teacher. People don't know about female bullfighters – Conchita Cintron, Karla de los Angeles, Cristina San Czech, these women know how to fight the bulls. We think fighters are only men but this is *mierda*."

"What is it?"

"*Mierda*? Bullshit."

"I'm still a pale European."

"The Cuban sun will take care of that," Ibbie said.

THE SKETCH ARTIST

"... the only trials to come to a good end are those that were determined to have a good end from the start..."
— The Trial

Policie Ceske Republiky
Prague

NOVAK DOLLAR was going on his twenty-eighth year as a sketch artist for the Prague *policie*. He started with the PCR when he was 19, right out of Professional Secondary School.

He was what people called a "Roma" child, a gypsy. Dollar had thick black hair and a trimmed black goatee. Once Inspector Kopecky overheard one of Kamila Nemec's friends tell Kamila that she would cut off her arm before she'd kick Novak Dollar out of bed. Both women giggled like a couple of 13 year olds. Many Romas ended up in special schools for the mentally disabled as if being Roma was a bewitched state needing correction. But Novak had a talent, something an average guy could admire. No one in the department had ever denied that. "You tell Novak Dollar a story and he'll paint you a picture." That's what people who worked with him said, the bigots and the non-bigots. You could despise fucking gypsies but you had to give *that* fucking gypsy some credit. People damn well would, too. So the other thing they said was, "You may

not like the man but you've got to respect the talent."
Nobody liked gypsies because most people had gone to
a train station at one time or another and had their
wallet and/or passport snatched by these *mali
bastardi.*

"How you coming along?" Dominik Kopecky said.

"Mrs. Lipski is giving me what I need." The gypsy
didn't look up from his sketch book.

Mrs. Lipski sat next to Novak on the edge of a dark
wood, high-back chair. She looked maybe late sixties,
early seventies. Minnie was describing the women
who'd sat on the park bench across from the Hoffmann
place the night of the murders. Minnie was a nice
looking woman, Kopecky thought – lean like an
athlete; muscular, too. Marathon runner was what the
inspector guessed. Her pretty white hair was brushed
soft and straight.

"One day I'm going to give that husband of your's
a run for his money," Kopecky said and winked at
Minnie.

"He'd pay you to take me."

"He's smarter than that."

"All sales are final," Minnie said; gave a phlegmy
laugh. "–That's what he'd tell you, the old dear. He's
not one to miss a beat." She's been studying the pencil
sketch Novak was drawing. Minnie said to the gypsy,
"Her hair comes up in the front like two horns. She
reminds you of the devil's daughter."

"The devil doesn't have a daughter." Dollar was
studying his sketch.

"It's an expression, *laska*," Mrs. Lipski said, *laska*
meaning love.

Inspector Kopecky knew these two had known
each other for years. Never got along. Never agreed on
anything. Minnie believed Novak Dollar was a godless
gypsy. Novak believed Mrs. Lipski wasn't in her right

mind. Each one had a lot of patience for the other's handicap – what good friends do – but Kopecky felt their whole friendship was a high wire act with no safety net.

"Where you live again, Minnie?" Dominik said, pulling up his swivel desk chair next to the old woman. One of the fluorescent lights above them winked on and off in no particular rhythm. "I know you told me, but refresh my memory."

"You getting the Alzheimer's?"

"I got the genes for it, *Matka's* side of the family," the inspector said; grinned at her, trying his best to stay friendly. "Her poppa had it. Alzheimer's, I mean. At the end, the guy couldn't tell you his own name. That's what I got waiting for me. What about you, Minnie? You got anything like that waiting for you?"

"Our family remembers too much," Minnie said. She was talking to Kopecky but watching Dollar sketch their Person of Interest. "My Saul can give dates and places," she said. "That's what I get for marrying a man who remembers 'the little things.' Our boys are like that, too – both of them. I don't want my family lecturing me on what I did three years ago. It's annoying beyond belief. Forgetful people are easier to live with, I'm sure of it." Then to Novak, "You got her looking cross-eyed."

"It's shading."

"She's cross-eyed."

"...another critic," Dollar said under his breath.

"Where do you live?" Inspector Kopecky said to Minnie again. He was looking over the gypsy's shoulder at the sketch. At first he had glanced at it to see if the woman in the picture was truly cross-eyed, but now he was studying the face. Kopecky didn't want to tell Minnie, but he was exactly like her husband and her boys. He never forgot a face.

"I live next door to the Hoffmann's," Minnie said. Her kitchen overlooked an alleyway and faced the Hoffmanns' kitchen window. "Sometimes Judita and I would wave to each other when we were fixing dinner." The older woman glanced up at Kopecky. "What do you do with the pictures?"

"Run them through an Interpol data base to see if we get a match."

"People can do that?" The old woman sounded amazed.

"It's an algorithm," Kopecky said. "–a computer programs that narrows choices. They got them for everything – GPSs, your favorite beer, combat scenarios. You name it and there's an algorithm. With Mr. Dollar's sketches, the algorithm looks at facial features, hair, what-have-you, and. eliminates data that doesn't fit the parameters."

"Listen, I have a confession," Minnie said, looking at her lap. Her voice had a quiver. "I saw this woman."

"Yeah, sitting on a park bench, you said. Across the street from the Hoffmann's."

Minnie stared at her lap. "Maybe it was a little more that than."

"...how much more."

"She was going through Judita's kitchen window."

WHAT A GIRL LIKES TO HEAR

"Quick, get the doctor. Did you hear the way Gregor spoke just now? That was the voice of an animal, said the chief clerk..."

— Metamorphosis

A Beach at Heaven's Own
Boca Raton, Florida

LOTTIE HANDED CUMMINGS a narrow, fist high glass of vodka; saying, "Straight, chilled, no ice? I think that's how you like it."

"Swarovski Crystal?"

"That's your brand, yes?" She lifted the bottle halfway out of her handbag just enough for him to see the label — $6,922.00 for that baby. "I got this particular vodka at the Maddox in London." Lottie had bought it 8 months ago. She liked to plan ahead. "I'm a Grey Goose gal myself," she'd told him. "Peasant stock, I like that."

They were sitting in matching mint green and white striped canvas beach chairs near the edge of the surf. That part of Heaven's Own beach was deserted, the sun starting to go orange along the horizon. Lottie had on a blond straw hat with a big brim and her Jackie O. sunglasses. Between the hat and the sunglasses every part of her face was covered but her nose, lips and chin.

"My God, this is just outstanding," Cummings said, looking at his chilled vodka. Then he nodded toward her handbag. "You got ice cubes in there, too?"

"You know us girls, I got the kitchen sink."

He took another sip and settled into his chair. His linen Bermudas were wrinkled, his beefy hairless pink legs crossed at the knee. "Give me an icy Swarovski vodka and a comfortable chair by the surf, and I can die a happy man."

"I'm glad you feel that way," Lottie said and patted his arm. She'd noticed that Cummings had brought a fat black leather pouch the size of a small gym bag. The bag lay on the white sand next to his chair. "What's in that?" She nodded toward the pouch.

"Tanning supplies."

"Or a weapon."

"The money's already in your account." He was staring at the cloudless sky, blue and turquoise ocean. "A bit too late for shooting, don't you think?"

"That's what a girl likes to hear." She kissed her palm and touched his cheek.

"A savvy business man stays honest," he said and took another sip of the Swarovski and smiled at the now half-full glass he held with a thumb and index finger. "That's all we have in the end, isn't it – our word, our character, our reputation? It's like a respectable line of credit. How we control our temperament is what separates us from the animals."

"...the animals." Lottie whispered; thinking about it, a second, two. "Yet..." She let the word dangle there.

Cummings stared at her. "–Yet what?'

"We shouldn't underestimate instinct."

Nodding slowly, he said, "It's a balance of sorts, isn't it? One without the other is never a good idea."

Lottie took the manila envelope from her handbag and handed it to Cummings. The man laid the unopened envelope of his fleshy tan knees. "I'm sure the company will be pleased to get these photos back. They're a big part of our current negotiations."

The vodka appeared to have made her employer more – what would be the word? More *amiable*. Yes, she thought. Cummings had accepted this glorious day, accepted her peculiarities, the hair that darkened her bare legs and arms, hair that curled down from the large straw hat and draped her shoulders and back. Lottie imagined him thinking of himself as a benevolent pet owner and she as his exotic property.

"You're not drinking?" Cummings said.

"The Swarovski is my gift to you."

"But I insist," he said, pointing his partially full vodka glass toward the neck of the bottle that peeked from her handbag. "Go on now, get yourself a taste."

She giggled; gave him a soft oh-*you* pat on his bare arm. "Trust me, hon, you don't want me tipsy. I become entirely too far too clever."

Cummings laughed and finished off his drink in a single swallow and wiggling the empty glass in the direction of her handbag. "More for me," he said. Lottie filled his glass. Then he said, "This is all very thoughtful of you, really. It's quite a chunk from your fee, isn't it?"

"It's the least I can do," Lottie said. "I appreciate your business. It's a way of making up for my sloppy first attempt. That's not like me. Ruins my professional standing, so-to-speak.

Consider my gift an apology."

The big man studied her, his eyes blinking slowly like a lizard in the sun. "You're a *very* hairy girl," he said.

Lottie's smile froze. The muscles in her face refused to do anything. "So I've been told," she said, her tone calm and even. "What can I say? God has a sense of humor."

"The whole hairy thing is sort of a turn on." Cummings was staring down at his glass, sniffed at the vodka and sighed with a barely noticeable shiver. "Recently I shared this thought poolside with some old bitch who told me it was a gay thing." Cummings looked at Lottie, the whites of his eyes bloodshot pink. She thought his eyes were out of focus. He said, "It's some type of condition, right, the hairy stuff?"

"Hirsutism."

"Yeah, that," he said. "Fucking fascinating, seriously."

"Maybe I will have that drink."

Lottie leaned away from him, her hand searching her big leather bag. The sun had disappeared behind gathering clouds. The ocean had turned calm, smooth and gray. She found her Beretta 92A1 with the silencer and pointed the automatic at Cummings. Too bad he hadn't opened the manila envelope and seen all the photographs of her middle finger. She'd gone to a lot of trouble.

"What are you doing?" He looked more bewildered than frightened.

Lottie shot him once in the forehead, a muted pop.

FRANZ'S THERAPY

part 3

"... I was a disinherited son, who needed constant reassurance about his own particular existence..."
— Letter to My Father

Oración a la Milagrosa Polyclinic
Havana, Cuba

FRANZ NEVER KNEW how to begin his treatment session. "I keep to myself," the boy said. "I've always been that way. I don't know how to start a conversation, I get anxious. But I'm good with people who pick a topic."

"You think there's a wrong topic?" Coro Acosta seated herself in one of the two plastic office chairs, Franz sitting across from her. Today she wore a colorful red and gold silk scarf about her head. It was fixed in front with a small, neatly tied knot. The uneven concrete floor had been scrubbed early in the morning and parts of the floor were still dark and wet. Lilac disinfectant was strong in the room. Dr. Acosta said, "Didn't you once tell me that happened with your father? You gave an answer he didn't like?"

"...yes."

"What did he do?"

"Locked me in the pantry," Franz whispered. He still felt embarrassed.

151

"–with those insects."

"...Yes."

"There's no right way to begin therapy," Acosta said. Her hands were folded and propped on her knees. Morning sunshine reflected off the tiny wet islands of the floor. "I know it's hard for you to just say what comes to mind. But that's the way we begin, okay?"

Franz was looking at the half open window, the sunlight on the peeling, pale blue window sill. "I have a new friend. Her name is Ibbie."

"You have a girlfriend?'

"I have a friend who is a girl, yes."

Coro Acosta stayed quiet.

Franz wasn't sure what to do next. He needed to say more but he didn't want anyone else but the doctor to know. "You don't tell people, do you?" he said. "I mean what we say is confidential, isn't that so?"

"You know our rule," Acosta said, studying him. "If you feel you're going to hurt yourself or others, I'd have to let the people know who could help us." She leaned toward the boy, arms resting on her knees. "Do you feel that way, Franz? Are you thinking of hurting yourself, or others?"

"...It's Ibbie," he said, looking everywhere but at Acosta. "She has the same condition as me, like my hand. I showed you, remember?"

Dr. Acosta stayed quiet.

"A bunch of kids in our school have it – ten, maybe fifteen. I don't know how many, exactly. It's on different parts of their bodies, arms and legs, their backs, their stomachs. Ibbie has it in her right eye. The eye looks like a greenish honeycomb, what flies have. Her girlfriend broke up with her last week because of it. They'd been going together for over a year. The girlfriend thought it looked too creepy."

"Have you thought about what you and your

friends have in common?" Coro Acosta said. "Besides the physical symptoms, of course." She was writing notes on a yellow legal pad and stopped to look at him. "I want you to think before you answer. You may not even have an answer now and that's fine. Think on it."

Franz felt his stomach go tight. He dreaded not having an answer, dreaded the "condition" that was changing his body and trying to control it. He'd seen photographs of people in a jungle village becoming insects. He saw faces shaped into screams. Franz had seen his Uncle Max go through the change, or partly through it. His uncle's feet, calves and thighs had shed pale skin for dark bone and spiked bristle. He had seen Max transforming on a toilet while taking a shit.

Franz couldn't get rid of that image.

"...what feelings do you guys share?" Dr. Acosta was saying. "Don't be afraid to ask questions. Again, I'm not talking about symptoms – I mean in your *lives*, every day things. What do all of you have in common?"

"I don't know about the other kids."

"Then find out, be curious," Coro Acosta said, smiling, She had a little space between her very white front teeth. Franz liked how she looked. Like an older kid, he thought. Like your babysitter, older than you but not all that old.

Immediately Franz felt his cheeks and neck go warm. He didn't get why so many feelings and thoughts embarrassed him. Now he was inspecting bits of dust turn in the sunlight.

"Everybody gets angry too fast," he said. "I know people who'd hurt you for no reason – just to see you scared." A quiver rippled along his back and shoulders. Franz found himself having difficulty catching a breath. "People get used to living that way, think it's ordinary. You can get used to horrible things, horrible people – I can, anyway."

"Your father, you mean."

Tears welled up and surprised Franz, hot tears smudging his vision. He used the back of his hand to wipe his eyes. "But it could be anybody, too. That's all we have left, the ways people mess with us. And what am I supposed to do? How do I feel okay with that?"

COLE READS
KARL'S DIARY

"... her gaze was cold, clear, and steady as usual, it was never leveled exactly on the object she regarded but in some disturbing way always a little past it ..."
— The Castle

Callejon de Hammel
Havana

HE COULD READ, and not just Czech but handwritten Czech. From the start Cole had been able to access sections of Max's consciousness as though these pieces were different parts of their same breathing, feeling, thinking whatever-you'd-call-it — *being*. He could remember

Max finding his brother Karl's diary under the nephew's bed while cleaning. How Max wanted to read it right then and there. But it was a chance he refused to take, like so many in his life, chances ignored and regretted. Cole had appeared about an hour ago in Max's empty bed, close to two-thirty in the morning. What the beetle found fascinating was his intense urge to read whatever the brother had written, words that didn't interest him in the least.

Moments ago he'd dragged the diary into the moonlight with his mandible, its appendages gripping the tobacco scented leather with a precision that surprised him. What would a young nephew think,

155

finding his uncle sprawled on the hardwood floor in beetle form? Cole didn't believe the beetle part of it would bother him. No, the boy would be more upset finding him reading a diary that was not his to read.

A quick look was all Cole intended. To do it while Franz slept quietly, deeply. Children were masters of sleep. Enjoy it while you can, he thought, holding down the diary pages with the dark slender hooks of his forelegs. Sleep will not come so easy later on, he muttered, more soft clicks than words.

Tuesday Evening
June, 2015

Yesterday our neighbor Kamila Nemec said she saw my step-sister Lottie sitting on a wood bench across the street at the edge of our neighborhood park. I almost soiled myself. I haven't seen Lottie and her drooling, snapping mouth since she ran away from home, age 12 or 13. She was always an angry little pisser, always afraid love wouldn't be there long enough to do her good. Or worse, she'd never get the share that was her due. Her "share" was all of it, of course. The child went beyond the expansive and ravenous bounds of greed into a vampirish persistence that cared for nothing but absolute satiation – to know her was to wish you didn't. She had been an embarrassing shit of a girl

Cole felt mischievous, amused. He knew the feeling was coming from Max. Then he heard the man's thought; a whispered voice saying, Lottie wasn't the only child who wanted more than I could give. Karl was a beggar, too. But our new sister was cuter than Karl. She had big, soft eyes and a sweet face. What's the expression? She could "play the room" better than my brother. That was her gift, God's gift to her. The girl got inside your head. Karl had muscular shoulder and thick legs. Karl looked as though he was born to protect other people. Protecting *him* never occurred to anyone. Now curiosity had taken the beetle. Cole gazed down at the diary, waiting for Max to reveal the page to him.

Mother had found Lottie in the alleyway next to our house, Karl had written. Someone wedged her between two garbage cans, wrapped in a wet, icy blanket. All I remember was a screaming, smelly baby who loved being the center of mother's world, and believe me, she clung to that center and refused to let go. She didn't play well with others; didn't share her toys.

Baby Lottie also never shut her mouth and never gave any of us a peaceful moment. She was the sort of creature who should have died. It's true. I see her as having made the inside pages of the *Prague Daily Monitor*, a photo of a blurry faced infant, red and frozen, icy lashes glued shut.

How better we all would've felt had she died.

We *tried* to save her, I imagined telling reporters. Pictures snapping, cameras rolling. Poor thing was beyond our meager prayers and skills, I'd say. Perhaps if one of us had been a great preacher, a man (or woman) able to tug on the heart of God, a man (or woman) able to pull God's attention away fromthe shootings and bombings of far more assertive religions than the spiritually blasé and unaffiliated like us. Perhaps we could have done away with the ideaof God favoring the one dark sheep espoused by mega congregations on Holy Rockin' Rave nights. The more amazing the light show, the more God will notice your desperation and take pity.

In my fantasy, reporters shouted their questions.

"Did you find baby Lottie dead, or did you kill her yourself?" A perky young brunette woman from the local TV station wanted to know. "Had you at least *tried* to save her?"

157

"I was committed to saving her," I envision myself saying, my expression a mixed of sorrow and puzzled offense. Even as an adolescent I'd have known to get the most from this fantasized tragedy. "You know how boys are," I would've said. "We long for someone to protect. This is how we practice our future roles as breadwinners and pillars of dependability."

Had Lottie died from the winter and our neglect, I was ready to show myself as anyone but what I was, a hateful boy who'd once set her dress on fire. Yes, yes, I know what you're thinking, I see your judging eyes. How is he still walking the streets? Is he roaming the back wood for more victims? Let me tell you what I know better than my name. *Had* she died – by accident, mind you; never think evil doesn't have it's accidents – Lottie Hoffmann wouldn't have grown up and torn our world apart.

Cole found himself nodding, agreeing. When the beetle realized he felt the words in Karl's diary were factual, Cole stopped for a moment and wondered how he knew that. Max knows it's true, he thought. Then Cole thought, I can feel the man trembling. He's still afraid of her. That's it, isn't it? The man is still afraid of his sister, what she does, the danger in her.

FARR PHARMA VS. WOLF LADY

"To marry, to start a family, to accept all the children that come, and to help them in this insecure world, is the best any man can do."

— Letter to My Father

On the Court
Merion Station, Pennsylvania

HE WAS THE cleanest man Lottie had ever seen who wasn't a model or a movie star.

Breton Farr had trained his sweat not to intrude on his appearance, was what Lottie figured. He wore pressed white shorts and a white top. His hot little tennis shoes were so white her eyes would ache if she looked at them for too long. Right now the man was hitting balls on his backyard, red clay court from a RoboBall 855. Robo had a shotgun arm and the ball exploded out of its muzzle at 95.6 MPH every 16 seconds.

Ole Breton was working his impressive booty.

"I like your moves," Lottie shouted over the thump-thump of the Robo machine, her left hand curved like half a megaphone. She walked onto the court, waving a manila envelope above her head. *The* manila envelope. This wasn't the one with the amusing full colored photos of her middle-finger. No, this had close to every photograph Karl Hoffmann had stolen from Elijah Cummings – and thus Breton Farr – the Bug People pics in all their heartbreaking glory. A bystander could've heard bones snapping at every minor transition, the tug and pop, as the infirmed went from human to bug and back again. Lottie was telling him, "I would say you're going to be a rich man, Breton, hon, but that time has obviously come and gone. So let me just say, you're going to be a much *richer* man."

"I'm calling the police," Farr said. He'd stopped RoboBall 855 with his remote control. The man was standing on the other side of the net, arms dangling at his sides now, the handle of the racket captured loosely between thumb, index and middle fingertips. "You're on private property – *my* property."

"Fine, Breton, be a dick." Lottie gave the manila envelope another shake. "Why don't I just take these photographs to the *Philly Daily News* or *The Inquirer* or that other one *Philly.Com*? What's the better paper here in the City of Brotherly Love? Maybe I'll make copies and send them to everybody."

Before Lottie had started speaking, Farr had removed his cell from the pocket of his shorts. Her brief talk about newspapers put panic into the man's face. He let the cell slip back into his pocket.

"Wh-What photographs?" he said.

"I call them the Bug People."

"… shit."

"Oh good, I have your attention." Lottie gave Farr a big smile then pushed her tangled dark hair away from the sides of her face with her free hand. She wore her usual black latex biker outfit – skinny legs, skinny arms. She said, "Two million wired to my BVI account will secure both your material –that is, the photos – and a guaranteed end to my involvement."

Breton Farr moved to the edge of the net and signaled Lottie to join him. She took her time getting there. Lottie first noticed the man's eyes, a silvery green, the deadest fucking eyes she'd ever seen. She imagined him freaking out a lot of rich boys with those eyes.

"Now it's three million, Breton."

"*Excuse* me?" The extra million had pumped color back into his face. "*No*body's giving *any*body three –"

"Want me to jack it to four?"

Lottie watched Farr take a breath and compose himself. He showed her a brief, ever-so-easy smile. Then he said, "Explain how you came to three million?" His voice was unruffled, almost casual. "Can you do that much for me? Why do you think that envelope is worth that much money?"

"Because the world has changed."

"The world is always changing," Farr said, a gentle, dismissive wave of his hand. "It's what the world does. Con*si*stently. We all want to live in what we think was the best time, the most comfortable time – the fifties, the eighties, whatever's your favorite." Breton Farr rubbed the lenses of his rimless glasses with the bottom of his white pullover. "But the Arrow of Time doesn't stop to take in the view. Time doesn't settle down. It doesn't say, 'Oh, I love this place, let's stay here.' We adapt, or we die."

"Haven't you noticed the wounded?" Lottie was her *own* Arrow of Time, never swayed by another's agenda. She said, "Bandages have become the new fashion statement, Breton. Arms, legs, the spine – you name it and someone is wearing a designer bandage over it. It's remarkable, really, how we've crippled ourselves over the last five or so years. Access ramps have become our new normal."

"...the wounded?"

"Mr. Innocent," Lottie muttered, picking up one of the pale green tennis balls. She stood and said, "See,

I'm betting you've already worked up a cure for our bug people. I'm also betting it's a cure that doesn't quite cure. And don't tell me you haven't figured out the profit margin. I've even thought of a new logo for your company. 'Farr Pharmaceuticals – why have a cure when you can get a refill.' How's that sound?"

"You have a bank number," Farr said, all matter-of-fact.

"I'll wait while you call it in."

THE MARVELS OF CROSS-REFERENCING

"Was the lawyer trying to comfort K. or to confuse him? K. could not tell, but it seemed clear to him that his defense was not in good hands."

– The Trial

Policie Ceske Republiky
Prague

KAMILA NEMEC FROM records had just brought Inspector Kopecky the DNA report on the two long strands of dark hair found at the Hoffmann crime scene. The report included the photo of a perp match taken five years ago for drug possession with intent to distribute.

"I know this woman," Kamila said, laying the file on the inspector's desk in front of him.

"You know her, too. I mean, how does a person forget someone like that?"

"So case solved?" Kopecky said, trying for a laugh. He realized it had come out a bit too snotty.

"You're being dismissive again."

The inspector looked up at her. "*Again*? I do that a lot?"

"It's one of your least charming habits," she said, motioning him to open the file. Kamila was leaning over Dominik Kopecky's shoulder. He could smell her perfume, a sweet flowery sent. Lilac, maybe. Not too much, not too little; the woman always knew how to walk that fragrance line. Dominik had been thinking about asking Ms. Nemec out for the last three or four years. Nothing complicated – lunch, a drink, a movie, a nice walk on a pretty day, not all at once, of course. Non-threatening shit.

"I *do* know this woman," the inspector said, studying the photo. "Her marijuana days, yes?"

"It's an old picture."

"–Five years, not that old," Kamila said.

"It's a long way from selling weed to a double homicide."

"Okay, you got that right."

Inspector Kopecky stood, holding the photograph beneath the florescent lights. "Jesus, always with the hair. The girl had some sort of condition. Lottie Hoffmann, that's her name. The girl was a terror. We'd have these long emotional talks. She'd cry and cry and promise me she'd never do whatever-it-was again. Usually, it was stealing some little thing – cheap jewelry, a sweater, a pair of gloves. Later, she started selling weed. She could always get to me, you know? I own that, believe me. I was a sucker for this kid. But I also arrested her. I can't begin to tell you how many times I arrested the girl."

"–Twenty-three."

"Shit."

"Yeah, twenty-three arrests, Dominik."

"Really? *That* many?" The inspector shook his head. Kopecky knew it'd been a lot of arrests, but 23 times was more than he remembered. "You try to have faith in people."

"Don't torture yourself," Kamila said, patting his shoulder.

"We're talking a double murder." The Inspector looked up from the report and photo. "Let me torture myself a little."

Kamila Nemec was perfect as far as Kopecky was concerned, sincere, intelligent, a wondrously precious face. Big eyes, bow lips. She also had magnificent breasts and a *derriere* a man could worship. But a man doesn't ponder dating a woman for three or four years and do nothing about it. How long do you need to think about that? Fact was, nowadays he liked being alone. Two earlier marriages and numerous girlfriends had seen to that. Women loved the idea of a cop husband/boyfriend until the guy started missing birthdays and anniversaries. Thank God he didn't have children. Bad enough he has to disappoint adults. Still. People have needs.

"You think she could've killed her brother and his wife?" Kamila said, sitting on the metal chair at the side of the inspector's desk. The chair was painted mint green with a black seat.

"Who knows what's in a person's heart."

"–Ex*actly*. People are capable of anything." She said that with the conviction of personal experience. He thinks, what are you capable of, dearest? What's more fascinating than a person who speaks with confidence about secret things? Then Kamila said, "I apologize. That sounds so I don't know – jaded."

"I was going to say 'intriguing.'"

"You're kinder than I deserve," she whispered, but did not look at him.

This is why Inspector Kopecky loved Kamila Nemec. Maybe not love, not in the strict sense of the word, perhaps in the general sense. What detective doesn't thrive on a good mystery, the prettier the better? Kopecky wondered if the wives and lovers of detectives were always mysterious types addicted to the chase, each adventure in need of an unexpected and rewarding conclusion. He imagined saying to the captured Ms. Nemec, "You see, my dear Kamila, you've been caught by the master. Game over."

"I'm such a bad girl," she'd say in his fantasy.

"–Very, very bad."

"Perhaps such a bad girl deserves spanking." Her suggestion, one that caught his breath.

The inspector decided to stop his daydream before the thing went off in an unrecoverable direction, nothing worse than hobbling around work with a boner.

"Does Lottie have it in her to shoot her brother and his wife?"

"People are desperate nowadays," Kopecky said, clearing his throat and getting serious. He turned from his computer and looked at her far too charming face. "I don't know why they're desperate but they are. Maybe we don't have the security we once had; you know, in our jobs, our family life."

"How about crazy strangers coming into our country and killing us."

"That, too."

KID/ IN THE BED

"Be patient! It's not quite as easy as I thought. I'm quite all right now, though. It's shocking, what can suddenly happen to a person!"

— Metamorphosis

Callejon de Hammel
Havana

IBBIE HAD BOTH pride and fear in her voice. "I became a beetle last night," she'd whispered to Franz as if her transformation had been something holy like the Pope blessing her or telling her how hot she was. "I'm in my bed," she's saying, "You know, naked and all – I really like that, being naked. It's, I dunno, *freeing*. You don't need to worry about sheets pulling your undies. Don't you hate that?"

Franz said he did.

They were sitting on his bed, backs against the clean white wall, Ibbie playing *Bloodborne* on her PlayStation, a game Franz had vowed to play until the day he died. But lately he couldn't play it because of his bandaged hand. Ibbie was doing a good job with the game. She'd died only three or four times during the last hour. Franz also noticed her eye patch was absent. This afternoon the girl's eye looked perfectly normal. He had noticed the same with his uncle, the changes came and went. That hadn't happened with Franz.

167

There were days when his hand looked improved, less dark, less bony and hooked, but his "condition" never totally vanished.

"Give it time," his uncle had said. "Eventually, it'll come and go." This gave Franz hope. Every morning he'd glance down at his hand and hoped all would be well and every morning he was disappointed.

"So *any*way," Ibbie said, "I thought I was dreaming. I mean I could hear my body crack. My shoulders, my legs. God, talk about pain. And I'm thinking, shit, I got to wake up. I'm praying it's not real, you know?" Ibbie's thigh kept touching Franz's thigh as they talked. He was trying to concentrate on the game and what his friend was saying but he had this massive hard on. The girl was still playing the game and talking. "Cause my auntie is like a heart attack waiting to happen. She gets anxious about everything, a lot of it with good reason. But she's all I got and I hate seeing her upset. If my auntie dies, I'm a total orphan."

"Yeah, I get that."

"Oh crap, I'm *sorry*. I don't know what's wrong with me. I've got *no* brain." Ibbie was obviously embarrassed, Franz could tell. "I forgot about your parents. You and me, huh? I guess we're lucky to have relatives."

"Forget it." He nudged her with his shoulder in a playful way. When people felt bad for him, it took away his everyday life. It left him on the outside. He felt less regular, less like a person who fitted in. "Look there, it's the boy with the dead parents," people whispered. "That's the boy whose parents got bullet holes in their heads." Then Franz said to Ibbie, "It's just what happened, that's all. People die constantly. It a nightmare but it's not so special, anymore."

"You're an orphan like me, right?" She gave him a quick look, her hands still working the game pad controls; still focused on the game. "That's right, isn't it? You've got just an uncle like I got just an aunt. I mean if they die, too, what happens to us?"

"I've thought that."

"See, this is what goes through my mind – having nobody, being an orphan." Ibbie stopped and muttered "fuck" under her breath. Her *Bloodborne* character had just died. She said, "I was totally alone last night. I'm changing into this thing, this *insect*, okay, and the pain is killing me. I'm telling myself, 'Don't yell, don't yell,' and I got my face buried in the pillow. I can't breathe, you know? But that's my choice, isn't it? Either I yell for my auntie and she get's a heart attack, or I suffocate."

"...God," Franz muttered; not sure what to do, he rub-patted her back.

"Exactly."

Two men had started to argue below Franz's bedroom window. One of the men sounded like Uncle Max. The other man, he didn't recognize. Franz went to the window and looked down into the courtyard. An older man was talking to Max. The man clung to a wood crutch, his right leg and right arm bandaged. Wounded people were everywhere now – maybe a better word than "wounded" would be "altered" or "changed." And it wasn't just old ones. Lots of people Franz's and Ibbie's age had bandages. He saw them everyday on the streets and in his school. Nobody said anything, either. Once in awhile a bandaged girl or boy he didn't know would nod to him in the hallway or in a store. Like there was a kinship between them. "You're not alone," that's what the nod said. "I'm the same as you," it said. Franz always nodded back. At first he did it to be polite. Then he did it because he felt relieved. Thank God I am not by myself in this, he had thought. "Thank God, that person is suffering, too." Franz didn't want to feel that way but that's how it felt.

He wasn't only one with a "condition."

The old man that was talking to Max had just collapsed on the sidewalk in front of their condo. Max knelt, propping the man's head and shoulders on his bended knee. The old man began telling Max something in Spanish.

Franz glanced at his bandaged hand. "This never goes away," he said to Ibbie as he looked back outside at the two men. "Uncle Max's stuff goes away, sometimes," he said. "You're stuff goes away, too."

"You don't want it to go away," Ibbie said.

"Of course I do."

She kept staring at her game. "The next time it comes back, it'll brings more."

"Maybe it won't come back," he said.

"Shit, Franz. It *always* comes back."

A BODY TOO FAR

"What you said meant that I should do something which we both considered to be extremely dirty; and that you wanted to be sure that my body didn't carry any of the filth home ..."

— Letter to My Father

San Francisco de Paula
70 km. Outside Havana

SHE WAS A child trying to hold back a big surprise. Aria Maloof had never seen her like this, so little girlish, all giggles and being coy. Who would've guessed her Lottie could still be a chirpy thing with a secret that couldn't wait?

"What is *wrong* with you," Aria said, half amused, half uneasy. She didn't like not being "in" on Lottie's secrets. "Pardon me. Are you *drunk*?"

"I had a vodka at the airport. Two, actually."

"You don't drink *air*port vodka," Aria said.

Lottie lifted the Swarovski Crystal far enough out of her black leather bag to show the label. "Does that look like airport vodka, hon?"

"Jesus, Lottie. We don't have that sort of money."

"We do now." Lottie grinned and wiggled eye eyebrows Groucho style. "Guess how much is in our overseas account as of yesterday before closing?"

"*Your* account."

171

They were sitting under the green and gold striped awning on their front porch. Aria poured wine into her glass from a small bottle of Pinot Noir on the wicker table. Her dark hair was pulled back off her shoulders. The day had become hot and damp early on and hair stuck to her skin was the least favorite of things. She wore a ragged white t, cut-offs and no shoes.

"Our account," Lottie said. A breeze twirled dust from the narrow main road and sent the dust across their porch steps. "It's *our* money. It's always been our money, baby. You know that. What's wrong here? Try not to turn all Ms. Grumpy on me."

"How much money and where did you get it?" Aria heard her own suspicion.

"You mean who did I have to kill?"

"That, too," Aria said, though not as loudly as she wanted to say it.

"So we're having this conversation again." Lottie wasn't asking a question.

"Farther Jorge thinks we need a, you know, heart to heart."

"The *priest*?" Lottie had that are-you-nuts tone. Curled hair draped her skinny, tan shoulders. "You're kidding, right? What is this, like Egyptian humor?'

"I don't *have* a sense of humor."

Lottie thought about that one then nodded. "Okay...all right. What possessed you to talk about our business with a priest?"

"I knew this wouldn't go well."

"You talked to somebody about our business. My business." Lottie had no emotion in her voice; the words cool, even. Aria had been with the woman long enough to know this was an attitude a person needed to take seriously. Lottie said, "Talking to people about our business is never a good idea. I did tell you that, didn't I? We did agree to keep our business to ourselves?"

Aria knew it was too late to back away from it. "See. I *told* Father Jorge, I said, 'Father, you don't know my friend. You cannot talk to her.' That's what I said to him. And look, *there* it is – you and this tough bitch attitude. Like you're Al Capone, or whoever. *Whom*ever. It's always been your way, or nothing. You know I'm right." Aria felt her heartbeat go heavy and push against her chest. The palms of her hands had become damp. She hated the way she showed fear. Her fear was just one big fucking parade. "Damn it, Lottie, how do you do it? How do you stay so calm all the time?"

"I can walk away," she said. She'd said it right off. Then Lottie added, "I could walk away from my own life, if I had to."

"I couldn't do that."

"That's why I'll beat you every time."

"You'd leave me?" Aria whispered.

"You know the answer."

Aria did know the answer. It wasn't that Lottie didn't love her. Or loved her less. Or loved her at a distance. Or had other lovers on the side or waiting in the wings. None of that had ever been true. Lottie was as loyal and caring as any committed partner. But there were events in Lottie's past that had taught her a lesson others had missed. School had been out for most of us on the day they taught that lesson, the day Lottie Hoffmann learned nothing is permanent in this world. Really learned it. Learned it as a baby hanging out among the trash cans in a snowy alley filled with garbage and decay and the stink of those things. Whatever or *whom*ever you love will come and go, period, nothing complicated here. It was how the world worked.

"Now I gotta go have a talk," Lottie said.

"With who?" Aria already knew. "What do you mean 'have a talk,' what sort of talk?"

"What the fuck you think?"

THE SECRETS OF ESTEFAN CRUZ

"... with you the purity ended, and with me the filth began."

– Letter to My Father

Callejon de Hammel
Havana

THE BANDAGED MAN lay on the gray velour sofa in Max's living room. Franz and Ibbie had carried him up two flights of stairs and placed him there; Max supervising, of course.

This was an important friend, Franz could tell. He'd never seen his uncle this nervous. Like Franz and Ibbie were plotting to dump the guy out the next available window. His uncle's lack of trust left the boy feeling depressed.

"Don't worry about it," Ibbie whispered.

"I feel like a criminal. My uncle doesn't get upset, not with me, not with anybody." Franz was using a paper towel from the kitchen to wipe the sweat from his face. Ibbie had just finished a glass of water. They were walking back into the living room to listen to Max and his friend.

Then Franz said, "I've never seen my uncle like that, all nervous."

"The old guy looks pretty out of it," she said, another whisper.

When Franz and Ibbie reached the living room, the mix of shadow and sunlight showing dust in the air, Max was sitting on the edge of the sofa near his friend. The friend had bruises about his eyes. His bandages were gray and soiled. A small, thin man with sharp bony angles, Franz remembered how heavy the old guy felt when he and Ibbie were carrying him up the steps. I must be really be out of shape, the boy thought.

"...the pharmaceutical company that burned down our last place," The bandaged man was saying. He had a Cuban accent. His voice was weak and Franz was having trouble hearing him.

"...our Venezuela community. I almost died there. *Farr* Pharmaceuticals, that was the name. My people found their name quick enough, let me tell you. The bandages on my arms are from the burns. Forgive the smell."

"Don't worry about such a things," Max said.

"You're a good friend."

"This is Estefan Cruz," Max said to Franz and Ibbie. There was a reverence his voice.

"Dr. Cruz is a physician, a hero among heroes. He's found our cure. I've seen friends who have our condition, friends who've remained symptom free for two years, three years. Scholars will put him in the history books, Franz."

"You flatter me." The old doctor grinned; silver outlined a dark tooth. "I can assure you I am still vulnerable to this hideous malady. I *believe* we have a cure, but the fire made me to leave too soon. These bandages are not just for my burns, I still have our affliction, but I'm sure it's because we had to leave or burn to death. We left too soon, I am sure of it."

"I believe in you, Estefan."

"Thank you for that, dear Max. I know I am right."

"Nothing can dissuade me," Max said to him. "It

hurts my heart too see you like this, Estefan. It's a sin. You who have given courage to all of us. I couldn't have stood up to these horrible men who burned your village, believe me. Or spend my time in a jungle, for that matter. I'm too dependent on my creatures comforts – a simple warm bath, a familiar bed with a favorite pillow. What can I say, Estefan, I'm a shallow man, too dependent on modern conveniences. My morning coffee, for example. My emails and messages, my TV – especially the news. It's the first thing I turn on in the morning."

"You live dangerously," Dr. Cruz said. It didn't sound like a joke.

"I'm as bad as the people I can't stand."

"Yes. My problem, too."

"I turn on the TV thinking who killed who today," Max said. "Who's winning the good fight. And so many fights. What moron is going to tell me climate change is bullshit again. Or worse, it's *natural*. American TV is the best for that sort of thing – science haters, religious zealots, gun nuts. Yesterday I saw an older black woman from Texas telling a reporter how she can't go grocery shopping without seeing pistols strapped about the bellies of crazy white people. Then I start getting pissed. Everyday it's like that. I'm always angry. I simply want hit someone in the face, just punch somebody, *any*body. It's embarrassing."

"But don't you see, my friend, this is the problem." Estefan Cruz reached up and touched Max's cheek. "The world has always been a violent place. Unfair, disappointing. But now it's inescapable, isn't it? Worse, it's like a drug, like heroin. We watch, we listen, we take sides. Empathy has become our grace and our enemy. Nothing is left to ignore. And there are days when the anger is insurmountable."

"Most days I want to stay in bed."

"It's killing us," Estefan said.

Franz stood behind his uncle. He felt Ibbie take his hand. Her skin was warm and damp. She stood close to him and he could feel her shoulder trembling, something irregular but there. Franz leaned toward her and whispered, "Do you want to go?"

Ibbie shook her head, her eyes not leaving the old man on the sofa. If the boy thought about it, he felt nervous, too.

"There must be a place people could go, " Franz said, blurting it out. "–A new place they don't know about. The pharmaceutical company, I mean. A place like your last place."

"That's why I'm here," Dr. Cruz said.

NO CONFESSION TOO GREAT OR SMALL

"If he had been alone in the world it would have been easy for him to ignore it, although it was also certain that, in that case, the trial would never have arisen in the first place."

– The Trial

Iglesia de San Francisco de Paula
San Francisco de Paula

EMOTIONAL SUPPORT, THAT'S what Aria had told her. "I know you love me," Aria said. "I'm not saying I don't know you love me. I do. But you don't need me the way I need you. I hate being that person – the one who needs the other one more than the other one needs me. Why am I always that person? Why can't *you* get suicidal, occasionally?" Once Aria had taken a handful of some sleeping pill or other – who can remember a name, the pink and green ones – and Lottie had to drive Aria to the hospital to get her stomach pumped. "Oh I get what's going on," Aria said. Yesterday they'd had this discussion on their front porch. "Believe me, I'm *not* a stupid person, okay? If I act up all the time, that reassures you, doesn't it? You can be little Miss Cool as a Cucumber, that's what you can be."

"Did Father Jorge tell you that shit?"

"What if he did?" Her chin actually jutted out on that one.

"You don't tell people our business, hon."

"...I know ... I know." Now Aria had a head down.

"*Do* you? I'd never guess it."

Lottie Hoffmann wasn't a person to leave loose ends untied. Who's to say priests or friars or whatnot can't be gabby bitches? These were *not* the days to trust clergy. These were not the days to trust – period. Had there ever such days?

The Church of San Francisco de Paula was an ancient gray stone gothic that overlooked Havana Harbor. Tiny inside, Lottie thought, now glancing about the place. This was her first step into anything religious since the last time her mother took her to synagogue for the high holy days when she was twelve or thirteen.

"Do you wish to take confession?" The priest was tall, six-three, six-four, stoop-shouldered with a narrow cleanly shaven face. Then he said, "I'm free, if you need my services."

"Are you Father Jorge?"

"Do we know each other?"

"–Not yet."

"Well I look forward to it," Father Jorge said, and nodded toward the confessional. "I'll only be a minute, child. Why not get yourself comfortable?"

The confessional was shadow and wood. It smelled of aftershave, cigarettes and something else, something vague and slightly pungent, perhaps nothing more than the sweat of the guilty and the concerned. Lottie sat on the hard bench, a small slatted window to her left. She'd placed her black leather handbag on her lap. Concealed at the very top of the open bag was her Beretta 92A1 with silencer.

Lottie couldn't recall ever shooting a clergy

member – no priest, no rabbi, no minister, not one person of the cloth came to mind. She thought killing this type of individual was bad luck. Like shooting God by proxy, or certainly God's minions. Who the fuck knew, really? All of it was bullshit, anyway. She imagined lightening snapping and popping overhead.

"Aria isn't the only hysteric," Lottie muttered. Oh I *get* it, what's not to get? The world is a scary place. We need that special someone who can conquer our enemies and always protect our frail lives. We need an afterlife so we can meet up with our family and old friends. And above all else, we need to continue *our* journey. Isn't that the name of this tired old tune? Don't let me rot, don't let them dig up my unadorned bones. Please, dear God, let me continue *my* journey. All about me, me, me.

"...begin, please." Father Jorge had just seated himself on the other side of the small slatted window, the smell of cigarette smoke wafting in with him.

"That you, Father?" No sense killing the wrong guy.

"It is. Sorry for the delay."

"Is there a particular way you'd like me to start?" Lottie said.

"Aren't you Catholic?

"–Not a practicing Catholic."

"Okay, fine," Father Jorge said right away. "All are welcome. It's not my job to decide who deserves God's ear. Let the Creator pick and choose, I say. I don't presume to know His tastes, His likes, His dislikes. I gave that up years ago. God goes out of His way for people who most of us think are a waste of time. But that's the Creator; always with the surprises." Father Jorge began coughing, a sticky, phlegmy cough. After settling down, he told Lottie, "What can an old man say? It makes the job interesting."

"I like you, I see your charm, how you might effect

others in your parish. Your sincerity, your humility, it's infectious. You have a true calling, don't you?" Not waiting for an answer, she said, "I suspect a man like you knew exactly what you wanted to be from the very start."

"My mother knew," Father Jorge said, an almost inaudible sigh of resignation. "Personally, I don't think she could bear seeing me married. No one argued with mother, of course. Not me, not my bother and sister, especially not my father. He feared her, too – all of us longed for our peaceful moments."

"I bet she's proud."

"Perhaps." His voice coming softly between the wood slats of the window that separated priest from parishioner. "But her pride comes from victory, I think."

"Where would the world be without strong willed women?" Yes, Lottie truly liked this priest. Not many men would tell a stranger how their mothers arranged and guided their lives.

Lottie even felt a twinge of sadness for the man. Then Lottie said, "I guess she's passed now."

"Mother?" He gave a little snort. "The old gal just celebrated her ninety-eighth birthday last month."

"How fortunate you are, Father."

"I wonder if the Lord has forgotten her."

An overhead wood fan moved slowly and silently above them. It stirred the warm, damp air of the confessional. Lottie noticed bits of dust at the edges of the dark wood slats of the small window. She wanted to say how the man needed to give attention to his housecleaning skills. But she didn't; she didn't say anything. Her kindness bewildered her. Get on with it, she thought. "Do you know who I am, Father?"

"Aria described you very well."

"My hair, no doubt," she said.

"Yes. And so slim. Lovely." Father Jorge adjusted his robes, or that's what it sounded like to Lottie. Then he said, "Too bad they don't let you smoke in these things."

"I won't tell, if you won't," Lottie said. She heard the click of his lighter and a full-throated inhale. The blades of the wood ceiling fan sliced through pale blue smoke. "You impressed me. Father. I'm sure Aria didn't spare the slightest detail. Yet here you are, sitting with me. How does one explain that?"

"As you say, it's my calling," Father Jorge whispered.

"Do you understand why I'm here?"

"You don't like sharing secrets," he said.

"I ... I apologize, Father."

Lottie removed the Berretta from her handbag and immediately sent four bullets through the wood divider that separated them. The silencer gave off no more than a muted *pop-pop* sound.

She heard his body hit against the other side of the tiny confessional then thump ever so softly to the carpeted floor.

CHANGER

"He lay on his armour-like back, and if he lifted his head a little he could see his brown belly."

— Metamorphosis

Callejon de Hammel
Havana

HE HAD TRIED to scream but nothing had come out except a sound like dice rattling in a loosely closed fist. That was his big scare in the dark. He also tried turning on the nightstand lamp but he didn't have his hands anymore. What he *did* have he didn't know how to use. Black, bristled hooks – what does a person do with hooks? Franz thought. He wanted to call Ibbie and tell her that what had happened to her had just happened to him.

Wanted to talk to Max, too. Franz needed to tell his dear uncle how he'd finally joined The Club. Ha, ha, ha. Franz's feelings were flying everywhere. Part of him felt terrified but he also felt the way he had the night of his father's birthday after sneaking a glass of champagne – both dizzy and exhilarated.

"Nothing wrong with a little bubbly," his father had told him. "*Never* play the fool, though. People remember the fool. And they'll remind you forever."

Get out of bed and wake Max, Franz thought. He imagined discussing their mutual anxieties and strategies bug to bug, so-to-speak. Franz also imagined himself and his friend Ibbie traveling with his uncle and Estefan Cruz to the place of The New Cure. That was Mr. Cruz's name for it.

Franz knew his mom and what she would've said to him on this night, her one and only child. He knew that even a nightmare wouldn't have ruffled her demeanor. She'd have moved toward him with a gentle expression and her boundless, calming spirit. Dr. Judita Hoffmann could weather any crisis.

"It was a gift, a calling," Franz's father had once said of Judita. "I trusted your mother from the start. She has always been a diamond among the stones. You're a lucky boy, Franz. Don't you forget it."

Tonight he thought about how his mother might have comforted him.

"You are still my beautiful boy," Judita would have said.

"I'm a freak," he'd say; a frantic whisper, no doubt.

"It's just your condition." Her voice always reassured him. Franz felt her fingertips on his cheek. "You remember our talk? Everybody gets conditions. That's what it means to live and breathe. We weather our conditions; we pray for the best."

"Look at me."

"Talk to your uncle now," she'd say. "Who better to help you? Hasn't he suffered, too? We all take chances, Franz. We hope our chances aren't reckless."

He pictured his mother embracing him and holding him close to her. He could feel her warmth and smell her lovely skin. Franz wanted to bury himself in her comfort and sob in the safety of those arms. He wanted to sob with all his breath and all his life. He'd sob for himself and the ones who'd suffered before him and the ones who had yet to suffer at all.

But where would they hold one another now? Was there room in the grave for two? Franz could never picture his mother in any place other than a hole in the ground beneath her chiseled gray tombstone and the mowed grass that showed the seasons. Angels and demons were never mentioned by either of his parents. No heaven, no hell. His mom liked to tell him that life was what you were given and what you made of it, and death was nothing at all.

"Do something with your one and only life, Franz," she'd say. His mother had said that a lot. "Make your days count for something," she'd said. "Be thankful for the ones you've loved and the ones who have had the good sense to love you back. And be thankful for the stars, too. They have given you at least as much as your daddy and me. Most of all, remember that you're one of the very lucky ones."

What would you say about me tonight, *matka*? Franz thought. Am I still one of the lucky ones? He was on his back and rocking to and fro, building up momentum and hoping the wood floor wouldn't break his shell or his twig-like limbs. That's when Franz rolled off the bed and landed on his back.

"...*shit*," he muttered. The word came out as a tired clicky sound. The next four or five minutes were spent doing more rocking motions until he rolled again onto to his four feet, or two feet and two hooks, or maybe four hooks – his body was a complete mystery to him. By the time he was right side up he needed a nap. Who can live like this? he thought. Not this boy, no how, no way. "Please let this be temporary," Franz's whispery clicks were to no one in particular. "Ibbie's change was temporary. Maybe mine is also temporary."

"Well your Uncle Max's condition was temporary," his mother said, always very supportive. "–*And* his friend Mr. Cruz. The condition does seem to come and go, doesn't it? Very good news for all concerned." Then she said, "I'm sure you'll be back to your old self in no time at all, my darling boy."

"Mama? Is that really you?" Franz was trying to

coordinate a four-legged walk down the shadowy hallway toward his uncle's room.

"Do you have me in your heart?"

"I think about you everyday."

"Then I'm here."

"No you aren't," Franz said. He wanted to shake his new head to emphasize the point but it was a new head attached to a new body and he didn't how to operate things. "You're dead and I'm alone," his words coming out too quickly to censor, or the clicking noise he used to make his words. "...and you're not here"

Franz was glad she wasn't real. He didn't want his mother to see him like this; to hear his weird noises. His mother was dead and in the ground. He'd seen the young caretaker use the brass handled cranks to lower the coffins of his parents into their fresh graves. Franz had thrown a hand full of dirt on each one. After the service, the boy had also watched the caretaker begin tossing the two mounds of dirt back into their perspective holes, covering the people who'd defined the boy's life. The truth was, Franz was alive and his parents were dead and they'd be dead forever.

"Come here, Franz." His Uncle Max was standing at the bedroom doorway. The man was wearing what he usually wore to sleep, white boxers and a sleeveless T-shirt. He was skinny with dark hair on his arms and legs, not as much as the Wolf Lady but hairy enough. Max knelt down on one knee and held out his arms. "You're going to be fine," his uncle said, his voice quiet and gentle. "Come here, Franz. Let's talk about what we're going to do."

WHAT IS WRONG WITH YOU

"... she seemed to be of another class, although of course illness and weariness give even peasants a look of refinement."

– The Trial

San Francisco de Paula
Outside Havana

NOBODY KNEW THE killer but Aria; so she believed. "What did you *do*?" Aria said to Lottie, the sort of furiousness that bubbles just below the surface of ordinary words. "Did you think I wouldn't find out? Are you that stupid or that charmed by yourself that you'd think I couldn't put two and two together? You killed a fuckin' *priest*, for godsake." Now the anger had gone from below the surface to lathering every word. "You *killed* Father Jorge. And don't tell me you don't know what I'm talking about, or start treating me like some crazy person. *You're* the crazy person. *You're* the person who gets her soul condemned to hell every five damn seconds."

Lottie was seated at the mahogany table in the dining room. Plastic baggies filled with 5 or 6 insects per bag were labeled in black felt tip pen and lined in rows in front of her, all done alphabetically. She was preparing new specimens for display. Sexy new bugs for the walls, she liked to say. Each insect had been pinned to a white felt background and labeled. The labels were written by hand, the whole presentation placed eventually in glass and wood frames. Most displays held a maximum of 4 bugs.

"Can't you see I'm busy?" Lottie said. She had on her silk gray kimono, the cuffs and edges rimmed in pink. Her dark unmanageable hair was drawn back tightly and held together with 1 inch thick, red rubber bands. How long that would last was anybody's guess.

"Are you even human?"

"Depends on who you ask," Lottie said, intent on her work. "Obviously this morning I can count you for a 'no.' But why don't you and I exchange arguments then let me get back to my work in peace. Go ahead. Beauty first."

"I-I can't believe you." Aria looked about the dining room as if seeking approval from an invisible jury.

"Really? That's your argument?"

"You *killed* Father Jorge."

"*We* killed Father Jorge."

"I didn't *kill* anyone!" Aria shouted, arms stiff at her sides, her fists pressed together like hard fleshy balls. "*You're* the murderer. *You're* the one who walked into his church and killed the man."

"Our business is our own. Did you think I was kidding when I said that?" Now Lottie looked up. "Have I *ever* been an amusing person?" She didn't wait for an answer. "The sanctity of the confessional has its limits, dear thing. A mass murderer who goes into a confessional and says, 'Well, Father, I did it again. What can I say?' He's not walking out of there. Or he's not walking far. It's like you've never heard of the greatest good. The greatest good for the greatest number – John Stuart Mill? Ring a bell?"

"I'm not educated like you," Aria said. She heard her own shame, her poutiness.

"I'm not educated like me, either. I read."

"Maybe you just need stopping." Aria mutters these words as if wanting to say it without being seen. A hit and run.

"Pack your stuff," Lottie said, pinning one of the dried beetles to the white felt backing of another display case. Then she pushed away a flop of curled hair on her forehead and glanced about the dining table for the current beetle's label. "I don't feel comfortable with you, anymore. Pack and leave, dear – neither of us is young enough or willing enough to change our ways. I'm sure you'd agree."

"Just like that?" Aria couldn't believe her.

"Yeah, like that, exactly. I can't trust you." Lottie's voice was matter-of-fact. "And please don't turn us into a drama. You wear me out. What do you expect me to say? 'Gee, I made a mistake' killing – *allegedly* killing – darling Father Jorge. What was I thinking?' Or how about, 'don't worry, I'll devote the rest of my life serving the poor and less fortunate.' If you're hoping for shit like that, then you don't know me. All these years and we're strangers. Listen, Aria: what I do is what I do. Life isn't as complicated as you'd like to think. But here's what bothers me, I don't ever seem to meet your whatever, your expectations. So you should, excuse me, get the fuck out."

" ...I have no money," she said, close to inaudible.

"Open an account. I'll wire you money."

"You think I want your money?" Aria said.

"Fine. Starve."

"Yeah, you'd like that."

"Here's what I'd like to do with you," Lottie said. "I'd like to kill you right now. Put a bullet in your noble, unforgiving brain. Every instinct I *have* is saying kill this bitch. But, lucky you, I can't do that. You're my Island of Charms, Aria, my only haven. So perhaps it's not unanimous, not all my instincts want to put you down, I guess – call me sentimental. Let me also say, if you decide to do things you shouldn't do, to go places you *shouldn't* go, to talk to people that will make my life less than stellar, I will put a fucking bullet in that lovely head."

GOD'S OTHER CREATURES

"... I'm just getting out of bed. Be patient. It's not quite as easy as I thought."

— Metamorphosis

El Fanguito
Havana

IBBIE TORRES UNDERSTOOD why her beloved Auntie Yamy had locked herself in their one tiny bedroom – three whole days now. Understanding her auntie didn't help the situation. It still made Ibbie feel like a monster. Aunties were supposed to comfort you; tell you everything will be all right. *No se preocupe, querida*, they should tell you. Don't worry, darling. Aunties were *not* supposed to scream and run into the bedroom and leave you alone and scared shitless.

Ibbie knocked on the bedroom door again. She'd been knocking on the door since early morning. "Auntie Yamy?" she said. "I *know* you're there."

"... *tengo miedo*," Auntie whispered. I am afraid.

"Have I ever in my life hurt you?"

"... *tengo miedo*."

What was the expression? Like a broken record? Yes, Ibbie thought. She's like a broken record. And what was Ibbie supposed to do, anyway? How do you make a broken record play a different song; what were the magic words?

193

Yamy was the younger sister of Ibbie's grandmother. Both the girl's mother and grandmother had been caught in the middle of a gun fight and killed while walking to the grocery store on the main dirt road. Two innocents caught between rival gangs who were solving an injustice, that's how Auntie told it. Nobody remembered the injustice and nobody talked about the father. Most of the women in El Fanguito had only contempt for fathers. *Padre en el pene solamente,* many of the women said. Father in dick only.

El Fanguito was one of the poorer areas in Havana. If not for the government giving them food and medical assistance, Ibbie and her Auntie would have been lost to whatever fate brought them.

Ibbie hadn't moved from her spot in front of the bedroom door.

"Tell me what to say, Auntie." Ibbie had never felt more alone. Without her Auntie Yamy there was no one to help her through this awful *lio*, this mess. "What secret words can I say that will calm you? What words can show you my love?" Ibbie said. "Listen to me, even though my outside changes, my inside stays the same." Then the girl leaned her ear against the door and knocked softly. "I'm scared, too. Can you hear me? I know what's happening to my body, but I don't know *why* it's happening. Understand? *No entiendo.* But I'm the same person, okay?"

No answer.

"Auntie ... hello?" Feeling her bones crack and reshape themselves was the worse pain she'd ever felt in her young life. How strong the images and feelings were in her memory. Ibbie didn't know what was worse, seeing herself transform in the bathroom mirror or feeling it. There was blood, too. Blood had gone everywhere. It oozed out of her skin and flecked itself across the stucco walls and dirt floor of the apartment. Ibbie thought she was dying. Like an angry animal had pulled her limbs from her body. New parts had replaced old parts and her body became a stranger. She had no idea how to work it. That evening Auntie Yamy had opened the door to the bathroom, took one look at her niece and ran from the room as though hellhounds were nipping at her sweet old ass.

"Come back, Auntie!" Ibbie had shouted. Help me! Please help..." But the words came out in frantic clicks, a metal on wood noise.

Auntie Yamy had shrieked, *"Eres el diablo!"* You are the devil!

"You hurt my feelings, Ibbie said.

"*El diablo* has no feelings! Only tricks, only tricks!"

Ibbie had begun scaring herself with thoughts of a life without her auntie. There was good news: in less than 2 days she'd returned to her old self, her skin bruised everywhere – neck, torso, legs, arms, simply everywhere. Ibbie felt exhausted, a sinking balloon leaking precious air, her energy nonexistent but surviving. She had laid curled on the dirt floor of their tiny apartment, sleeping, groaning and becoming herself again.

"Come and see what I look like," Ibbie now whispered to the closed bedroom door.

"Give me back my niece, *el diablo*!" Her aunt wouldn't quit.

"I *am* your niece."

Maybe it was time to leave.

Part of her saw leaving as an attempt to stay sane. She also wondered if the rumors of a cure had some truth, or enough truth to see for herself. When Ibbie imagined leaving home and her whole body would tremble. She'd always thought she was a decent person. But how does a decent person abandon her family? It filled her with shame her each time it came to mind. And there were many *good* memories – let's not forget our blessings. The day they moved into their little apartment, Ibbie painted the bedroom and bathroom doors a bright blue, Auntie Yamy's favorite color.

They were *very* happy then.

Her auntie always made them a favorite Cuban recipe, the Moors and the Christians, *Moros y cristianos*, black beans and rice. Yamy liked to cook and was good at it. The black beans and rice were always served with fried bananas.

Now Ibbie knocked on the door and said, "Listen, Auntie, we should be celebrating my healing, how I've over*come* this terrible affliction. I don't even have to wear that old eye patch you hated so much. My eye is better, too. Open the door and look at my eye, Auntie. It's a miracle. The angels have protected your niece who loves you so very much. What do you think of that? Isn't it wonderful news?"

Silence.

"Cook us your *Moros y cristianos*," Ibbie said. "How does that sound? Cooking always made you happy."

Silence.

"...Auntie?" she whispered. "Don't leave me. Please. Who do I have but my Yamy? You and me – hasn't it been so for all my life? Don't push me away."

THE CALL

"It's best not to overlook the tiniest details. Besides, I really want to help you in some way, however modest my help might be."

                     – The Trial

Policie Ceske Republiky
Prague

DOMINIK KOPECKY FELT ... well ... confused. He couldn't multitask the way he used to in his twenties and thirties. "*Who's* this again?" He was sitting at his desk, the phone tucked between his ear and shoulder while looking at his computer screen. Kopecky needed to finish a report he should've finished yesterday afternoon. "...hello?" He wasn't sure if the woman was still on the
line. "Who am I speaking to, ma'am?"

"Do I have to give my name?" She had one of those ethereal, flower child voices. Wasn't she way too young for all that – free love, brown acid, Jimi Hendrix? Hell, Dominik was too young for all that. He pictured the caller, her with her head tilted slightly, draped blond hair hiding one eye. Then she said, "I don't like giving out my name."

"Think of it as an act of good will."

"Is this confidential?"

He hated that question. Yes, it was confidential until he needed it *not* to be confidential. Such a promise had a high number on the bullshit meter. How does a person explain that? So often an event can

197

become a life or death moment, and at that point promises get overlooked. Saving a life most always had a free pass to the front of the line.

"Unless you tell me your name and why you're calling, I can't do much," the inspector said. That was true enough. The other question concerning him was, could this caller be cooperative; how much of herself could she risk if it all got tough and many times it all got very tough. He said, "These are the simplest questions I'll ever ask you. I mean why call me if you can't even speak your name?"

"I've never called the police."

"Fine, I'll be gentle," Kopecky said.

"Listen, this is *long* distance." Now she sounded pissy. The flower child had exited and a woman with a hard, bullying voice appeared. She said, "You know Cuba? Fidel Castro? Cute cars of the fifties and sixties? Socialism? I'm calling from fucking Cuba, bitch boy. How's that for commitment? I'm spending *my* good money."

"*Hey*, easy—"

"Hey, 'easy' shit. Arrest me, asshole."

"Okay, I'm hanging up," Kopecky said. Fucking women.

"I know who killed the Hoffmanns."

Okay, he thought, I'm not hanging up. He'd found strands of Lottie Hoffmann's hair at the crime scene. Kopecky wanted to hear a collaboration – something about Lottie's character; a few recent crimes, if any. And if Lottie had done other recent crimes, were these crimes like the Hoffmann crime?" He needed to build a case.

The inspector waited. He looked at the half-finished report on his computer screen. He wasn't sure how to make contact with the person on the other end of the line. Maybe he'd have to just wait her out. Take a breath, he told himself.

"You still with me, sport?"

"I'm here," Kopecky said. "Look, I don't want to keep saying, 'Hey, you.' At least give me a first name. Give me something."

"Rose."

"Okay, good, good. *Rose.* Rose, it is," Kopecky said. Her name was Rose like his dick was a flower pot. "Let me say, my name is Dominik, okay? Call me Dom, okay? Reciprocity is good for the soul – my opinion, anyway. I'm guessing you agree." He didn't wait for an answer.

"The Hoffmann crime, that's as serious as it gets. Somebody does a crime like that and I think, well, this isn't the first time. I think, it's gotten easier for him or her. They can do it and sleep at night. They're not like you and me – not that I'm a sleeper. I don't know about you, but if I get a couple of hours I'm lucky."

"Poor you," she said.

"Well if you're sleeping the night, you're the exception."

"Did I say that? Who said I sleep at all?"

"Exactly. Most of the time I'm up three, four o'clock in the morning reading some bad f-ing – *sorry*, long day – some bad mystery. See, I think our killer hasn't been like you and me for a long time, that's what I think. Maybe that person was *never* like us. Some of these people start early, you know? Kids, just kids – loners, what-have-you, anti-social types. You know anti-socials, right? I'm talking the real thing. Setting fire to animals, that type of thing. They belong to some other club, Rose. And, believe me, nothing you or I would join."

"Oh, I joined," the woman whispered. "Not that I knew, I never knew – suspected but didn't want to know. I've been with this person for many years. Do

you understand how difficult this is for me?"
     "I do now," he said.
     "...so what's next?"
     "Sit tight. I'm on my way to you."

FRANZ'S SESSION
part 3

"... you scarcely showed yourself during the day, and so you made an even deeper impression on me, and I could never get used to this."

— Letter to My Father

Oración a la Milagrosa Polyclinic
Havana

DR. ACOSTA SAT across from Franz, a yellow legal pad resting on her skinny, pressed together thighs. She flipped through her notes a page at a time. "Okay, I think you've done well, adjusted to your new situation, your uncle, school, made some friends, but I haven't heard much talk from you about your parents." Coro Acosta knew that people shy away from feelings and thoughts involving the death of loved ones. The feelings are simply too painful. Children have an especially hard time. Franz had lost both his mother and his father. The psychologist knew the emotional devastation of such an event; knew it personally. Maybe not both parents, but her dead mother wandering Coro's apartment was bad enough. Then the doc said, "I'm not sure I like the idea of you going off to some jungle in the middle of your treatment. No one can run away from their feelings for very long, Franz. Our feelings can turn up at the strangest times. And one way or another, they do catch up with us."

"Uncle Max is going, too," the boy said. There was

a pleading sound to his words. "Things are getting worse for me, Dr. Acosta. Uncle Max said there's a place where people can get better.

Why wouldn't you want me to get better? I told you about my changes. You think I want to go through that again and again? Have you ever felt your bones breaking?"

Dr. Acosta knew she had no counter argument against feeling her bones breaking. "No, thank God, no," She told him. "I don't see how you survived, to be honest. But I'm so glad you did. Maybe that's my only argument, the one argument I feel to my soul, Franz. And because I think you're such a nice kid, such a *good* kid – a person who's gone through more terrible crap than anyone your age has a right to go through – I want the world to pay attention to you. I want the world to go your way."

Acosta saw tears drape the boy's bottom lashes and trail his cheeks. "Can I come back?" he said, looking at the slant of the concrete floor. "When I'm finished with everything, can I come back and tell you what happened?"

"I hope you will." She did, too. She heard it in the sound of her own voice.

"You would've liked my mother," Franz said. He was still looking at the smooth, uneven gray floor. "I always knew she was there for me. You couldn't fool her, either. She was a doctor, too. She could look at a person and see what was wrong and how to fix it. When my mother first saw my hand, I could see the worry. She loved me a lot."

Coro Acosta knew her patient had just given her the highest compliment. Franz sensed the same love and concern from his therapist as he'd felt from his mother. "You would've liked my mother," the boy had said. "She was a doctor, too." Dr. Acosta knew the boy's loving mother and his therapist were bound together. She had earned his trust.

If the therapist listened to the patient, it was hard to lose the right course. Therapy worked like a sailboat looking for a good breeze. If the therapist made an intervention and the next association out of the patient's mouth was how his or her father used to beat him senseless, the therapist may want to rethink what he or her had last said. That was not the case today. Coro knew her patient trusted her treatment.

"I'll always be there for you," Dr. Acosta said, her voice soft, loving. In the beginning of her practice, she'd had a difficult time detaching from her patients, allowing them to leave the nest and find the type of life that suited them. Coro dealt with these losses over and over again. Only with time did she understand the mother's difficulty of opening her hands and releasing her babies. Acosta said, "This is the hardest part of my job, Franz. It's taken me awhile to learn that people always feel better when they find out they can care for themselves."

Franz looked up at her and grinned. "My mother liked to say, 'Let's see what the body does.' She told me that a million times. She'd say, 'Our bodies always know best, Franz. My job is to just get them on the road. I help them start thinking for themselves.' That's what my teacher taught me.' I'm glad you to do that, too," he said. "You are like my *matka*. She always told me, 'Let the body find its way.' That's true, isn't it?"

"–For our bodies and our selves, yes," Dr. Acosta said.

"... I'm afraid, you know."

"Yes. I'd be afraid, too."

"I can't imagine you afraid, " he said, looking at her.

"You think I'm braver than you, is that it?" She

thought about it for a moment and shrugged.

"I can't say yes or no. My bravery is always a surprise. But I'm shocked when I don't run away."

She glanced over her notes again; then looked up at him and said, "When you found yourself in the bathroom at school, ready to fight that boy, did you think you were brave?"

"He dragged me there."

"You could've run."

"I'd have been too embarrassed," Franz said, looking down at his lap. He became quiet and thought about the fight some more. Finally he said, "But if everybody wanted me to fight and I thought fighting was a bad idea – you know, thought it was wrong – and walked away, that would have been brave too."

"Now you're catching on," Dr. Acosta said.

ARIA DISCUSSES HER FOOT

"... There's always something new to listen to,' and he licked his lips as if news were meat and drink to him."
— The Castle

Hospital Popular
Avenida de Esperanza
Havana

FATHER JORGE HAD told her to see Estefan Cruz. The doctor was a friend and would know about what had begun to darkened and misshape her left foot. The *Hospital Popular* was very old and the gray walls and the ceiling were cracked. Aria could see concrete beneath the worn black and white linoleum floor.

"He died, you know," Dr. Cruz said. "A nicer man never lived."

"I ... heard."

"Who kills a priest? What sort of individual?"

Aria was sitting in the doctor's small office beside his old mahogany desk. Books and medical research papers covered the desk, all of it color-marked and tabbed. Apparently Dr. Cruz was in the middle of reading many things. The walls were painted a deep rose color and the paint was peeling, both walls and ceiling. Two overhead fans made a clicking noise as the wood blades turned above her.

On this already hot and humid morning, Dr. Cruz

was wearing a white long sleeved shirt buttoned at the wrists. Who does that? Aria thought. At first she wondered if the doctor wasn't a drug addict. He wouldn't have been the first doc who needed to hide his track marks.

Then she saw the tops of his hands were burned, his skin bright pink, skin stretched and folded in odd directions. It's a wonder any of us make it out of childhood, she thought. His scars remind her of the overwhelming randomness of tragedy. Anybody, anywhere, anytime – it was an on-going mantra she kept close to the chest.

"Father Jorge was my friend," Aria said, her voice practically inaudible. She was looking at the worn linoleum floor. "This is terrible beyond words. I don't mind evil people killing one another. You live that way, you die that way. I may sound, I don't know, inhu*mane*, or whatever, I don't care. But when you murder someone whose entire life was dedicated to others, I can't help feeling shocked and angry."

"Shot to death," Cruz said.

"I'm aware."

"–In a con*fess*ional. Imagine."

"Oh I can, believe me," Aria said. "The killer will get her due. The authorities are anxious to get this business settled."

"Her?"

"...or him."

The doctor studied her face, maybe looking for secrets. "You said *'her.'* Did I hear that? I know hearing has a way of kidding us as we get older." Dr. Cruz smiled. mostly to himself. He was an elderly man with a drawn, emaciated face. His cheeks and eyes were set back and shadowed. "I did hear you say 'her,' didn't I?"

"Men don't have a monopoly on violence," Aria said. "Believe me, violence is non-denominational."

Her shoulders were stiff and hunched and she took a breath and tried to relax. "Spend an hour or two in a woman's correctional facility. I spent many an afternoon visiting my dear friend there. It'll give you a whole new menu of nightmares. Men think they know women, they don't have a clue. There are women who'll cut you just to watch the blood run from your body. The women in those prisons think hurting you is just another art form."

"You've had experience with all that," he said, leaning back in his dark wood desk chair "I can see it in your eyes. You have the fever of the initiate. You've seen the nightmare, haven't you? You've seen the obsessed ... and you were very impressed. Yes, that's it, exactly – you were impressed, even horrified."

"Horrified isn't the word I'd use, Doctor."

"How so, tell me. Tell me about this violent woman." He leaned toward her now, elbows on the desk, his pink scared hands collected beneath his chin. "That *is* what we're talking about, isn't it? An experience with a specific woman?"

"To say 'horrified' is to suggests I was too afraid to stop it," Aria said. "That I would allow her mayhem to continue by doing nothing. And I absolutely did *not*, Doctor. If anything, I'd pushed her evil from my mind and I was slow to see my denial, that I admit. What can I say? This individual meant more to me than I care to express. To see her as a person who thought so little of life was difficult. Imagine seeing your love as less than humane. What person is strong enough to do that? I saw us as building a life together, paying for a home, buying groceries. I
saw us as the new American couple, June Cleaver marrying Wanda instead of Ward."

"–Instead of who?"

"It doesn't matter. The point is, I saw us as the all

American family. When I think about it, that was a pretty crazy thought." Aria stopped for a moment; wondered how she sounded to Dr. Cruz. "I didn't mean to go on. I'm not sure how I got started."

"You were avoiding telling me about your left foot." the doctor said, nodding to the flesh colored bandage seemingly coming from the depth of her shoe and wrapping about her ankle. "This is why you came to me, yes? That bandaged foot?" He nodded at it. Immediately, the woman withdrew her foot to the shadow beneath her chair.

"Dear Father Jorge was right. I can help you."

GUESSING
THE CURE

"The first response to his situation had been confident and wise, and that made him feel better."
— Metamorphosis

Callejon de Hammel
Havana

TWO SUITCASES LAY open-mouthed on Uncle Max's bed. The tan leather one was already packed. That one belonged to Franz. The boy's suitcase was new while Max's leather case had a weathered look, a case that had traveled to places Franz could only imagine. Early afternoon sunlight crisscrossed his the tightly made bed, the pale blue top sheet, the crisp white pillow cases.

"I don't see this is rocket science," Max said. They were discussing Changers, what Max called the people who'd go between insect and human – the condition and the cure. Changers in the first Venezuelan camp had achieved good results. "They hadn't stopped the transformations," his uncle said. "But the periods of staying human were getting longer."

"People believe the drug companies burned the camp."

"–Farr Pharmaceuticals, yes," his uncle said. "They wanted people to see them as the company with the cure."

"They have medicine to help me?" Franz felt a bloom of warm relief.

"Simple, isn't it?" Max said. He sat on the edge of the bed; patted the space next to him for his nephew to sit. "Take a pill and go live your life." His uncle smiled at a punch line Franz didn't get. Then Max said, "What if sacrifices had to be made to live a decent life? Renouncing our comfort zone is never easy, Franz. Imagine giving up all the things that bring you peace. What if the cure was scarier than the disease – losing the good opinions of friends as you travel to the dark and indifferent space of a cure? Could you get away from your TV, your phone, all the rest that brings you peace? That's what we're taking about, you know. You doing business in a different way."

"I like my phone," Franz said.

"Cures can be demanding."

"My friend Ibbie calls me, sometimes."

"It means we'd rather take a pill than walk away from our day to day," Max said. He was leaning back on his elbows now, looking at Franz who sat on the bed next to him. "That's our problem. We don't want to change anything. Most of us feel comfortable in our routines, even our petty hatreds. We just want a pill that will allow us to go on with our lives."

Franz could smell alcohol on his uncle's breath. Max had been drinking more these last couple of weeks. Sometimes Franz would get up in the night to go to the bathroom and see the lamp light in the living room. Max would be asleep in the recliner or the sofa, the TV on, the screen a white static buzz.

"You did a good job packing," his uncle said, nodding at the tan leather suitcase, the way shirts and underwear had been folded with smooth precision. "We don't need much," Max said. "Long pants, long sleeved shirts – good idea not to wear shorts in the jungle. We don't want to look like a creature's sunburned lunch, do we?"

"What'll keep people from setting this new place on fire?"

"None, absolutely nothing." The answer quietly given.

"Then why are we *going*?" Franz said.

"I think you know, yes?" Max said, looking up at the boy. His uncle had gotten up from the bed seconds ago and was now folding a pair of his own pants to fit into his suitcase. "I can't guarantee what will happen," he said. "I mean I *can* guarantee that I'll watch over you and take care of you. I'll do that for as long as you need me to do it; as long as my body and life are in decent shape. I think you're a good boy, and I love you. *Period*. End of story. But you have to decide how desperate you are, Franz – only you know. You've got to want these changes no matter what the challenge. That includes our own lives. It depends on how bad you want to survive."

"I want Ibbie to go with us," Franz said.

"The tall girl with the eye patch?" Max had stopped folding his cloths and stared at his nephew. The boy didn't know what his uncle was trying to see. "You like her, yes?" the uncle wanted to know but didn't wait for an answer. "—Very attractive, I give you credit."

"She's my friend," Franz said. He felt uncomfortable and didn't know why. "She doesn't have the eye-patch, anymore. She changed, too. Like us. And when she came back, that bad eye was all right."

"Nobody should take our trip lightly."

"Ibbie isn't that way," the boy said.

Max nodded and placed his already folded pants into his suitcase. "I like our place here, I like the people. But everywhere I go lately, I see ones like us. The bandaged ones – limbs and shoulders, mostly. And eyes, too. Like your Ibbie. What I'm saying is this: if the cure works, it may only work there."

"You mean we'll have to stay?"

"Maybe that's the cure," Max said. His uncle sat next to him and put a warm palm to his cheek. Then he kissed the boy's forehead and said, "Maybe we are like Columbus sailing into the new world."

KOPECKY TALKS TO INSPECTOR MARTINEZ

"I work for the court," he said. "What court," said I. And that's when he told me about the court. I'm sure you can imagine how amazed I was being told all this."

–The Trial

Comisaria de policia revolucionaria
Havana

EXTRADITION FROM CUBA to the Czech Republic wasn't as daunting as Kopecky had originally thought. He'd been dreading the whole conversation, his new Beat Your Head Against the Wall fantasy. But Lottie Hoffmann was still a Czech citizen, after all, and Inspector Freddy Martinez didn't mind a non-citizen leaving Cuba; and in this specific case, a non-citizen who was an assassin.

"If the lady in question was a Cuban," Inspector Martinez had said over the phone, "you and I would be having ourselves a different conversation. We like to take care of our own, *mi amigo.*"

Right after Dominik Kopecky's plane had landed at Jose Marti International Airport, the two inspectors met in the *Comisaria de policia revolucionaria*, a medieval, gray stone castle with a coat of arms above the entrance. The building reminded Dominik more of jousting knights than a police department.

"You sounded younger over the phone," Martinez said, a smile marred by one mossy green front tooth. Martinez was a short, obese man who wore dark leather sandals and an old blue pinstriped suit with wide lapels. The suit was tight on him, the vest straining at the button holes. The Cuban inspector said, "Europeans are such pale people."

"A product of past sins," Kopecky said, his half-smile quickly gone. Diplomacy first and foremost, he thought. "We are cursed, indeed. Yet we must muddle through, something learned from our friends the Brits." The Prague inspector's expression stayed friendly but business-like.

"We're truly embarrassed by our person in question, our Ms. Hoffmann. She's both troubled and dangerous. A blight on your benevolent good will, I'm sure. I wish nothing more than to bring this killer to a lasting justice."

"One of our priests died two days ago," Martinez said. He reached for one of the manila folders on his cluttered desk; flipping slowly through its pages. The dark wood desktop was worn and scarred. "–Found in the confessional, no less. Shot four times, twice in the temple. Imagine." Martinez continued to look through his notes. "Now I've started wondering if this could be your Ms. Hoffmann's doing."

"I've no way of knowing, of course."

"Yes, of course."

"But thank you," Kopecky said. He didn't trust the way the conversation had started to go. "Believe me, I'll keep you informed."

"I'm sure." Martinez looked up from reading the folder. "Perhaps you could stay here for a few days. You need a little sun, yes? So pale. It's unhealthy to have such a complexion. You could think of it as a vacation."

"I've got piles of paper work,"

"We' all have paper work, Inspector." Martinez had started to read the same folder again as he nodded to the stack of other files in his desk. "Occasionally a person has to say fuck it I'm taking personal time. Don't you agree?"

Inspector Kopecky stood and brushed an invisible something from the sleeve of his gray suit coat. Martinez waved him to sit down without looking. Kopecky leaned his palm on the man's desk, staring at him. Waiting. Waiting. Finally Martinez looked up. Dominik wanted to leap over the desk and smash his fist into this asshole's perfectly tanned face.

"Is there something else?" the asshole wanted to know.

"Thanks for your cooperation," Kopecky said, and turned. The rotating ceiling fan had a faint tapping noise and kept time to Kopecky's walk across the room's white and black tile floor. The five other officers were busy at their typewriters or fat ancient computers and no one noticed him.

Freddy Martinez called to Dominik as he was about to open the glass and wood office door and begin his search for Lottie Hoffmann on his own. "Inspector Kopecky." Kopecky stopped, hand on the doorknob. "Extradition requires the cooperation and good will of the Cuban government," Martinez said in a matter-of-fact tone. "We don't want to embarrass the people of the Czech Republic by jailing one of its officers. So I need you to accept a reality – our country, our rules, it's that simple, amigo."

Kopecky knew his own short-comings. Admitted them. He'd list them to anyone who had the slightest curiosity. Patience topped his list. But having insight was one thing; acceptance, something all together different. He said, "First, don't give me this 'amigo' stuff. I'm not your fucking amigo. How 'bout this, though. I'll just let Hoffmann stay in Cuba and kill more of its citizens. Would the Cuban government like that? I could make it known to the media that I had in good faith offered my assistance to rid their lovely country of a woman who killed whomever and whenever she wanted. How'd you like to be in that shit storm?"

BREAKING UP
IS A BITCH

"... for years I was tormented by the thought that this giant man, my father, could almost without reason come to me in the night, and lift me out of bed, and leave me on the balcony: he was my final appeal, and for him I was such a nothing."

—Letter to My Father

San Francisco de Paula
70 km. Outside Havana

SHE'D ALTERNATED BETWEEN controlled reason and cursing and banging the door with her fists.

Now Lottie yelled, "It's my goddamn house, Aria! You hear me?"

"The whole town hears you," Aria muttered that to herself. Lottie's wife, lover and friend of God Knows How Many Years sat on the cool slate floor of the foyer, her back against the front door, thin tan arms wrapped about her legs. Then Aria said, "Leave while you can, ole girl. Don't make me call the cops."

Lottie gave an audible snort. "You would, too."

"—Bet on it." She heard the bravado and tremor of each word. Her cell lay on the gray slate next to her. For two nights she'd slept alone, and last night Aria had set the local police on speed dial. "If you're not gone in five minutes I'll call them – I'll call the cops, I swear to you. Don't think I won't ask for help."

217

"You broke our promise, " Lottie said, her voice a cold gentleness. "–Our *trust*. God, I can't believe you don't understand what I had to do, that you left me no choice – *you*. You broke the one rule we agreed on years ago. And by the way, I would *never* break our promises. Did Your's Truly ever break a promise? No, *no* I didn't, little miss, I didn't break that rule of rules. See, unlike you, Aria, I take rules seriously. What I did I did to protect us, *both* of us – and our sacred, blessed union. I killed your wonderful, dipshit *friend* because you told him secrets you and I vowed we would keep between us."

"Don't give me that shit," Aria said. She turned and stared at the double locked front door that separated them. "You killed Father Jorge – you killed my *friend* – and you did it to protect yourself. " Aria's tears felt hot and blurred her vision. Tears marked her face, and she tasted the salt at the corners of her mouth. She said, "You don't protect 'us.' This is about me always shutting up so you can do as you please."

"That's not true."

"It's *always* been true. You must think I'm a fool." Aria searched the pockets of her cut-offs and found a turquoise paper napkin. She pressed out the wrinkles with her fingertips, and blew her nose. "What did Father Jorge ever do to you? He was a *priest*, you terrible dope. I've been living with a crazy woman who kills priests."

"You knew how I earned a living,"

"Yes. Yes, I knew."

Aria felt her stomach cramp – of course she *knew*. A person cannot spend time with another person and not know where the weapons are hidden, the canvas gym bags of wrapped bills, the days and occasionally weeks of waiting for Lottie to return to her, the two and three days of continuous sleep that followed that return

– what sort of person can't put the clues together? What sort of person ignores all of that? Love and survival, Aria thought. Too many situations make fools of us.

"Let me in," Lottie said, whispered it. "I'm hurt to see you upset like this. It's an awful pain in my heart. To know I'm responsible. You're so alone, so I dunno, *vulnerable*. I'm not heartless, okay? You're not the only human being whose got feelings, Aria. Don't get all Ms. Sensitive on me. Are you listening? I have feelings, too. Okay? I have lots of feelings about lots of issues. I know I don't share *every*thing with you – I get that. I get that I'm closed off when I should be open – or what the fuck *ever*. I *get* it. Truly. Your complaints don't go unnoticed. I'm not as insensitive as you think, I see what I've done. But it's hard to redo the past, isn't it?

Hard to go back and paint a different picture. Impossible, really."

Silence.

"Are you listening?"

"I'm calling the police now," Aria said. She had her cell to her ear but it was hard to press speed dial. "I can't keep letting you do these terrible things. I can't pretend " Aria felt nauseated, her stomach tight and raw, an acid taste lingering in the back of her throat. She shut her eyes and took a few quiet, deep breaths. Get it together, she thought. You know she'll keep doing these horrible things. The woman has probably killed more people than I could possibly imagine. And you *know* she'll do it again. Aria said, "I can't pretend you have this secret job – like the CIA or the NSA, or whatever these people call themselves. Like you're some sort of hush-hush do-gooder. I won't pretend that, anymore." "I *protect* us."

"You don't protect shit," Aria said. "You kill people."

"Don't you do this, hon."

"I-I'm sorry." Aria pressed speed dial and heard the tones connecting her to the *Comisaria de policia.* The phone began ringing.

"Stop the call. Please do this for me. For *us.*" Lottie Hoffmann gave a thump against the door, a gentle, almost inaudible thump. "–C'mon, please, *stop* it."

Silence.

"...oh, hon. My dear, sweet hon."

Two bullets blew through the door and burrowed through Aria Maloof's ribs, cut into one lung and dug away a chunk of her heart.

GETTING TO THE RIVER

"I know that nobody likes the travelers. They think we earn an enormous
wage as well as having a soft time of it."

—Metamorphosis

Jose Marti International Airport
Havana

THE TRIP FROM Havana to Belem, Brazil was 11 hours and 43 minutes with two stops. That would just get the four of them to the Amazon River. Estefan Cruz figured another day and a half managing the currents. "The new camp's out of the way," Max said, grinning at Franz and Ibbie.

They were sitting on plastic row seats, Franz and his friend still taking in the airport, its high, vast ceiling crisscrossed with thin metal tubes that had the look of a giant spider's web. A strip of bright red circled the room and indicated the various ticket counters below it. The floor was a buffed gray marble.

"I hope Auntie Yamy'll be okay," Ibbie said.

"You didn't tell her?" Franz's feet were propped on his tan suitcase.

The girl scrunched her shoulders. "I left a note" She gave a quick nervous smile. Ibbie slumped in her chair. She wore a sleeveless white blouse and jeans, her long skinny legs crossed at the knee. The heel of her leather sandal was loose and snapping a rhythm against her bare foot as she talked. "I didn't want to get into it with her. My auntie can be a *very* nervous person. Old people believe in the spirits —angels and demons, like that. You can't talk to them about anything unusual. I'm serious, they're *not* cool with it. I mean they start, you know, mumbling stuff to Jesus."

"Chicken," Franz joked and gave her arm a soft bump with his shoulder. He wanted to make her smile but he didn't know how to go about it.

"Auntie got very scared when I changed." Ibbie looked at the polished marble floor. She hesitated before saying, "It was like I'd lost her. Like I was a stranger. Auntie said *el diablo* had me. Then she locked herself in her bedroom."

"It's good that you're going with us," Franz said. There was a glass window in front of them. A small white jet was taking off and the bright afternoon sunlight reflected off one of the wings. "It will give your auntie time to miss you," he said. "People think different when they miss their family. One summer I went to overnight camp. I liked it okay, I guess. On Sundays they gave us pancakes for breakfast. But coming back home was the best part. My father actually took me in his arms and hugged me and kissed my cheek."

Ibbie looked at him, studying his face. Franz thought he might have a bit of food stuck somewhere. "I think I'll kiss your cheek, too," Ibbie said and took her time with the kiss. Her lips were smooth and very soft, and Franz felt his face go hot. Then Ibbie settled back into her chair and looked at the airplanes on the other side of the big sunlit window as if nothing had happened. "I've never been on an airplane. Have you, Franz?"

Franz could still feel her kiss on his cheek.

Ibbie looked at him and grinned. "Have you ever been on a *plane*?

"What? Yes, I sat next to a fat lady." Franz felt his face heat up again. Nothing he said sounded right. "Actually I fell asleep and woke up with my head on her shoulder. She told me gentlemen didn't do that."

"Oh perfect," Ibbie said. "People love telling you what you should do."

Right away he thought of his mother. That had been the good thing about her, one of many good and kind things. When he was with his mom he'd *wanted* to do right. There were people who made you a better person just by being around them. Even his father behaved better. Franz liked remembering evenings when everybody sat on the living room sofa and watched TV, his father on one side, his mother on the other. A big plush sofa with a soft corduroy cover, he loved the feel of it. His father usually turned off the lights as if they were in a theater. The TV gave the room a calming silver and white glow. His mother liked the windows open on summer evenings. The breeze was most always warm and smelled of the clipped boxwood drifted in from their yard. His mom had also kissed him on the cheek – many, many times.

Franz loved TV evenings with his family. He liked becoming sleepy and stretching out, his head resting on his mom's lap, his stocking feet draped over his father's legs. Of course Karl Hoffmann had to first give his permission. You didn't assume anything with his father. "Don't assume with me, boy," he'd say. "Wait until I tell you it's okay. Never think people are your personal property. That's a *very* bad habit, believe me. Nobody is the center of the universe in this world. Nobody *owns* anybody."

"Oh, Karl," his mom would say.

"It's my job to educate the boy, Judita. I'm his

parent, too."

Franz had to wait until his father tugged at the boy's stocking foot. That little tug signaled it was okay to stretch out on the sofa, to drape his feet across his father's legs. That seemingly inconsequential tug signaled a good night.

Karl Hoffmann could be okay, then not so okay. Franz knew when the Not Okay part was coming. There were always clues. The Not Okay part had a restlessness to it. The Not Okay part was demanding and angry. The Not Okay part included drinking vodka and smoking his pipe in the living room and daring Franz's mom to look at him funny. One sided fights would break out. The quieter Judita would talk the louder Carl would get. Finally, she had to take the pipe from his mouth and the vodka from his hand.

"Go up*stairs*," she'd tell Karl. "Go on now, I'll get your medicine. You know what you're doing, my darling. We've been here before, haven't we? You're no fool. It's your condition. Each of my men has his own burden to carry. Good thing I'm here, nothing like having your own private doctor."

Karl did know what was going on, Franz was sure of it. Maybe his father had lost sight of it for a moment, but eventually he'd sigh and nod and relinquish his drink and pipe and lumber off to bed. Once his father had stayed up for eight days straight.

His father knew.

Now Ibbie was holding Franz with both arms, the two of them sitting in plastic row chairs at the Jose Marti International Airport. He couldn't stop his body from shaking, his shoulders, his legs. There was average embarrassment and then there was the Crawl Under a Rock and Stay There Forever type of embarrassment. Thank goodness Max wasn't around, he thought. At least he doesn't have to see me. Several minutes ago his uncle and Dr. Cruz had walked to the large window to watch the planes. Afternoon sunlight surrounded the men with flash and glare.

"Hey, hey," Ibbie whispered to Franz, the boy still shaking. "It'll be fine. You hear what I'm saying, Franz? It'll be *okay*." She'd been kissing him on his forehead and cheek. C'mon now, we've got to look out for each other. You help me when I get down, and I'll do the same for you. That's what people do. Am I right? My Auntie says people need one another in this tough world. C'mon, boy, you know I'm right."

Franz couldn't look at his friend. The shame felt overwhelming. His father used to tell him how women hated men who didn't take charge of a situation. "They expect it, Franz. And if you want to impress the ladies, you stay strong."

One night Franz had told his mom what his father had said.

"Maybe those women need to keep strong, too," his mom said. She'd just finished reading him another episode of *The Little Prince*. Judita Hoffmann sat on the edge of his bed, brushing strands of hair away from the boy' forehead. "We take care of others because we *want* to, Franz. Because we like them, or care about them, or love them. We don't do it for any other reason. And we certainly don't do it because its our job."

THE WOLF LADY AS A FORCE OF NATURE

"And just now, when he would have to act with all the strength he could muster, now a number of doubts of a sort he had never before known had presented themselves and affected his own vigilance."

– The Trial

San Francisco de Paula
Outside Havana

AFTER KOPECKY SAW the bullet holes he'd moved quickly to the right side of the front door and drew his weapon, a Smith & Wesson revolver. It had the look of a snubbed nose .38, an old school police special, but the inspector's revolver was a .357 magnum. It could put a hole in your forehead the size of a nickel and blow away the back of your skull.

Kopecky bought the weapon when he'd turned 45. He knew his reflexes were on the way out and he wanted to avoid a second shot.

"Ms. Hoffmann?" the inspector said. "Are you there?"

No answer.

"Do you know who this is, Lottie? Think back. You used to tell me I talked like a peasant. That I'd be better off selling fruit in the park than playing with guns. Does that ring a bell? 'How does a peasant become a cop,' you'd said. You were what – sixteen, seventeen?"

Nothing.

"I know you're in there," he said. He didn't know that at all. Okay, maybe 65%. "And by the look of the door, I'm thinking I'll find your friend in there, too. Aria Maloof?" He still thought Lottie had made those holes in the door.

"I visited the church before I came here." Kopecky paused and tried listening for any movement inside the house – not a sound. Maybe he *was* talking to himself. He said, "You killed a really popular guy. Everybody loved Father Jorge. The man was like a celebrity. No, I take that back. He was a *saint*, a man of the people. Like Pope Francis, that rare sort of guy – humble, giving, and you could tell him anything. That's what people say."

Again, the inspector waited.

C'mon, Lottie, he thought.

"Not your typical religious asshole is what I'm *try*ing to convey here," Kopecky said. "You know, where you have to live a certain way or the devil comes and bites your ass – that kind of incredible asshole." The inspector gave a little laugh, trying to connect with what he thought was on the other side of Lottie Hoffmann's bullet-hole punctured door. Then he said, "But you had to go and kill the man. Seriously, what the hell were you thinking? I always took you for a smart lady. But you go and put a bunch of bullets in him. Because that's what *you* do. That's how fucked up you are, isn't it, honey?"

Not a growl, zilch.

Kopecky looked out at the sand and dirt street, de Paula's main thoroughfare, dust whirling up. Two boys were running about the road and rolling an old tire back and forth between them. The sun was bright and hot and reflected off the shops and homes. Ripples of heat bent the air and at times it was difficult to see the boys. The inspector didn't want to lose them. He didn't want them disappearing in the sunlight. He liked hearing the boys play. They reminded him of when he was that age – how old? Nine, ten? The days he could nestle into the embrace of one parent or the other and forget the petty fights and wounds of play. Who the hell wanted to be alone now?

"I know you're there, Lottie," he said, close to inaudible, yet loud enough. He could hear the softness of his voice. "It's my job, you know – to find you, to stop you. Sometimes I don't mind the job. Other times, I do mind it. We're here today because I've failed you. All the years we've known each other. We go back too many years, all the talks, the promises. But who were we kidding, right? People are who they are, what other honest things can we say? Kopecky paused; thought, shit, is that it? Is that all you've got for her. "Listen, I'm sorry I wasn't smart enough to get it right for you, to get you into some other life."

Lottie Hoffmann was inside the house, Kopecky knew it; *felt* it. And she was very close to the other side of the door. You work cases for a few years and you get feelings, scenarios that are the truth or very close to the truth. He imagined her sitting on the floor and holding the dead body of Aria Maloof. He could smell them, that's what he believed. He could smell the blood and the frantic sadness. He could smell the desperation of perpetrators and the quiet decay of their victims. Kopecky pictured Lottie sitting there an inch or two from him, only a door with cracked burnt holes between them.

She was no more than a trigger-tap away.

"I don't want to kill you," the inspector said. "And I don't want you killing me. Either way it's not how I want it to go. Killing's what we do. We can't work shit out any other way. I refuse to believe –" he stopped. What are you doing? he thought. This isn't twenty years ago and you're a police officer, not a social worker. Lottie Hoffmann was a grown woman who killed people to solve her problems, and she'd been doing it a long time. The inspector spoke to her now, his voice commanding but with the right amount of benevolence. He'd been perfecting that voice for many years. "I'm coming in, Lottie. You and me, we'll have a talk. Okay? No weapons, no cowboy horseshit, all right? Lottie?"

Silence.

Kopecky shoved his firearm between his belt and the small of his back. Then he stepped out in front of the closed door, hand in the air. "Let's you and I agree, nobody shoots anybody. First we see if we can work it out. Then we re-evaluate. Right now we're just going to discuss things. How does that sound?"

AN OLD BEDTIME STORY

"Memories of his home kept reoccurring and filled his mind."

– The Castle

Remembering an evening
Prague

THE GENTLE ROCK and hum of the airplane relaxed Franz. He was looking out the small window with half-opened eyes. Max and Dr. Cruz were in the seats in front of him. They were talking but he could only hear a word or two. Outside the window clouds blocked then revealed the late afternoon sun. He glanced over at Ibbie who was in the seat next to him. Her eyes were closed, her head resting on his shoulder. It would be a long trip and Franz decided to shut his own eyes.

He'd been thinking about how his mom read to him at bedtime and thought about one night in particular. That night Judita had finished reading *Robinson Crusoe*. She sat on the edge of his bed, looking down at him. Franz couldn't keep his eyes open. The bedroom was a mix of silver moonlight and shadow. There was also a circle of yellow light from the lamp on his nightstand. The lamp's shade had watercolor paintings of tiny sailing ships.

"Let's see your hand," Judita said, meaning she wanted a look at his "condition" before kissing him goodnight. She undid the bandage under the yellow lamp light and examined his palm, backhand and fingers. His hand had narrowed, his four fingers dark and stitched together the thumb fused into the index finger. "This is going somewhere," she said, examining the hand. "I don't know *where*, exactly. But let's keep monitoring it." His mom once told him doctor's liked saying let's monitor something when they didn't know what the something was.

"Am I going to die?"

"You should charge one *koruna* a look." His mother turned his hand over to examine his palm. She traced his lifeline with her fingertip. "You have a very long life line, Franz. You know your *matka* used to tell fortunes in medical school. Yes, it's true. We doctors are very superstitious people. Many came to me on the eve of exams. "Will it go well for me, Judita?" they'd say. "Will I earn many *korunas* in my chosen specialty of gastroenterology?' one boy wanted to know. And I'd look very carefully at his palm – as I'm doing to your palm now – and I'd tell him, 'Oh, yes, riches await the studious."

"Did you see his future?

"Nobody sees the future better than your *matka*."

"Is that true?"

"Oh dear, dear Franz, of course not." His mother lifted his chin gently with her fingertips. "*Nobody* can see the future," she whispered. "–including your parents who love you very much."

On that night as she studied his dark hand, bringing it closer to the lamp light, turning it first one way then another, on that night Franz could see his mother's concern. He'd wanted her to dismiss his hand. He wanted her to say, "Don't waste my time with your silly worries. Don't you understand, Franz, I have patients with *real* diseases, *real* problems. I've no time for your complaints. Do you think I'd waste the money my family spent on my studies to indulge the fantasies of children?" Yes, yes, he thought, tell me I worry for no reason, that you've begun to find hands like mine tedious. Ho-hum, you think. Look, another dark little hand. How stupid, how ordinary.

That night Franz saw his mother's eyes glisten and go wet. He felt hot panic take him as they huddled in that island of yellow light encircled by shadow. Don't cry, he had thought, don't make this serious. What am I supposed to do with you crying? I want to forget my hand. I want to do normal things."

"I'm sorry, Franz," his mother said, kissing his cheek. She began rewrapping his hand in the bandage. "It's been a long day. This isn't about you, my darling. I lost someone today, a long time patient. It's never a good day when a doctor loses her patient."

"This *is* about me," he said, his voice quiet, his head bowed as he looked at his mom examining his gnarled hand. "I think it's getting worse."

"Are you in pain, Franz?"

"No, ma'am."

"Well that's good news, isn't it?" Judita didn't wait for him to answer. She'd just wiped her eyes with the cuff of her cotton sleeping gown. "Tell me if you feel this," his mom said, and pressed a red polished fingernail into the palm of his hand. "Do you feel that, Franz?"

"No, *matka*." The boy shook his head. He said, "I-I'm sorry." He hated disappointing her. "I can see you doing it, but I don't feel anything. What does that mean? Am I sick?"

"Do you feel sick, darling?"

"No, ma'am. I-I feel okay. I feel good."

Two days later Franz heard his mother talking on the phone with another doctor. Judita Hoffmann was saying, "My husband has showed me photographs. You would not believe them, Dr. Bloom. Pictures of people who've changed into – I don't know what to call them – *bugs*. It seems so disrespectful to call them that, but I've seen them with my own eyes. What frightens me is my son, he changes, too. I have seen so many of these people. Adults. Children. It doesn't matter. They look so vulnerable. Help me, doctor. Please." Franz heard the panic in his mom's voice. I don't want to lose my son."

AGAINST DOCTOR'S ADVICE

"We're talking about two different things here, there's what it says in the law and there's what I know from my own experience ..."

—The Trial

Havana Hospital

HE REMEMBERED HER face and the stink of the thing she was holding and how she looked up at him. As he became more and more conscious of his surroundings and saw his right knee was bandaged – throbbing now in a steady, gnawing way – Inspector Dominik Kopecky knew he was in a hospital and remembered the situation that brought him here. He'd taken a bold step into the woman's foyer, his talk unruffled and friendly, his hands raised, no weapon in view. Sunlight came through a nearby opened window, light crossing the floor, glistening on gray marble laced in gold. Kopecky had smelled the situation before he saw it, the shit and urine stench, the stench of skin on the edge of decay. He recalled thinking, it's been a day or two. After thirty-two years of dealing with dead people, he could tell the time of death by the smell. The inspector had seen Lottie Hoffmann's hair first. Who could miss that hair? Tangled, thick, long – like a *wilkołak*, a werewolf. Lottie's thin, very pale arms were wrapped about the body. She was holding the dead woman as if wanting to push the flesh into her own body and keep it there forever.

"I've come to take you home." The inspector's voice had a softness, an inevitability. Lottie didn't look at Kopecky. "You must have loved her very much," he said and saw her shoulder muscles tense as she held the dead woman tighter. "But your friend is gone now, isn't she?" Kopecky said "No one can bring her back, not even you."

"God could bring her back, if he wanted to."

"I didn't know you were a religious person," Kopecky said.

Lottie put her lips to the dead woman's forehead, a silent kiss lasting a second or two. Then Lottie said, "God can do whatever He wants." She'd begun to rock the body, whispering to it. "God can do anything. If it was your time then we can't argue that, can we? But maybe it was a mistake, baby. God could've had another life planned for you, something he needed you to do. That's possible, right? We need wait a few minutes."

"I'm guessing you've been here at least a day," the inspector said. He'd knelt beside her; saw two wounds where bullets had entered the dead woman's body – one had exited shoulder blade level, the other exiting at the small of her back. There might be more, bullets lodged in the body. Lottie could have shot her a couple of more times once she'd entered the house, or perhaps there were additional attacks that didn't leave such obvious clues as a bullet hole. He planned to ship the dead woman to the department's M.E. If the Cubans stopped him, Kopecky would find another way. The Cubans could kiss his hairy ass. This was his case, his perp, his dead body. "Lottie, look here," he said. Lottie swept the dark hair from her face, turned her head and looked at the inspector. "That's it," he said. "Good girl. You remember me, yes?"

"...Kopecky."

"Smart as shit, too," he said that to himself, grinning. He had an urge to help her brush the mass of hair away from her face but realized that would be a stupid idea. God knows how she'd view him touching her, a dangerous line to cross. Kopecky actually liked Lottie Hoffmann as much as any cop can like someone who kills people. The inspector killed people, too. He just killed the right people. Also, Lottie's Beretta lay on the floor close to her hip. There would be no way he could reach behind his back, pull the revolver from his belt, and shoot her before she shot him. Practical stuff. Finally he said, "Tell me why you killed your wife." When in doubt, do the obvious. "I mean, look, I know you loved her."

"She broke the rules," Lottie said within a breath.

"What rules?"

Silence.

"We've known each other forever." His voice was relaxed, even conversational. "Help me understand, I don't know what 'she broke the rules' means. I *do* know you're short on trust, so she must've meant a lot to you. What rules?"

Lottie Hoffmann didn't answer immediately. But Kopecky wasn't in a hurry. He knew how to wait. He also wished the Beretta was further away from the woman. The inspector was thinking, if I get close enough, I can kick it from her and wrestle her down. "...what rules," he said again.

"To keep our lives to ourselves." Lottie was looking at the dead woman's face, its closed eyes, its peaceful countenance. "Was that so much to ask?" She said, more to the woman than to Kopecky. "I would've done anything for her. It was hard telling her how I felt. I don't express myself well in that area — what-you-call 'intimacy.' I think a person ought to know how you feel. Why else would I hang around?"

That was when Kopecky made his move. What's the worse that can happen, he'd thought.

Much later, as he lay alone in the foyer with two bullets in his right knee, the thought was, how fucking stupid are you? Now he had to get out of Havana hospital. His room was bright with sunlight. Soon Lottie Hoffmann would be gone, if she wasn't already gone. He had to rid himself of all the monitoring wires attached to his body and silence all the digital noises that let nursing know if he was alive or dead. Kopecky would then hide somewhere until the triage team was called to the next emergency. That shouldn't take long.

ΛRE WE THERE YET?

"... then we stepped out of the cabin into the sight of all the people, I in your hand, a little Skelton, uncertain in bare feet on the planks, in fear of the water, and incapable of swimming like you ..."

—Letter to my Father

National Park Parima Tapirapeco
Amazonas, Venezuela

THE AMAZON KEPT splitting, dividing. It just went on forever, Max Hoffman thought. The last split in the river for Max and the others was the *Rio Negro*. He'd seen creatures in the earthy colored water. Pink, long-nosed dolphins raised their smiling faces by the longboat, snapping their jaws and making "feed me" noises. Or that was Max's guess. Ibbie and Franz threw bits of bread at them and immediately the dolphins caught and ate whatever food came their way. Max also saw small gray monkeys sitting in the sand near the shoreline. They watched as the longboat glided past them. Some monkeys leaped up and down and called to the boat with shrieks and squeals. Some raced the boat until they ran out of beach. "How long now?" Max asked Stephan.

"To the landing site, two hours," the old man said. "–To the village, another day."

"I've never taken such a long trip, Max said. "I feel

we've left the world behind, the familiar, what I've always counted on. It's unsettling, Stephan."

"Every meme you've ever known?" Dr. Cruz had one of those smiles people get when they see someone going through what they'd gone through. Not a particularly malicious smile, nothing like that, more of a "this too shall pass" smile. "You once told me your very life was responsible for your deep, abiding stress. You said it was a wonder you hadn't given up on yourself, lost your yourself to drugs, taken your own life."

"We'd been drinking, Stephan."

"Tequila, if I remember."

"We were so damn drunk, we fought over who'd get the worm." Max shook his head; smiled to himself. He was looking at the white sand and the dark leaves of the shoreline. Three bright red and blue McCaws flew over the longboat toward the shore. Max said, "You won, thank God. Swallowed that awful creature like a cookie from a jar. But you're right, old friend. My life felt besieged, by what I don't know – I guess everything, the sheer violence and stupidity of the world."

"And now?"

"And now I'm here," said Max. "Now I'm completely lost."

"You're with friends and loved ones. How lost can that be?"

"I do feel an odd relief," Max said.

"See? How can you resist such lovely magic?"

When they'd arrived at National Park Parima Tapirapeco, Max had to readjust his thinking.

The parks he'd known were a couple of nice meadows, a duck pond. Maybe a little zoo. When Dr. Hoffmann thought of parks, he imagined parents watching their young children sailing toy boats in a pond, feeding the ducks and geese. Near them would be a stand with a grinning old retired guy, probably supplementing his pension by selling hot roasted peanuts in little brown paper bags. Max also imagined a playground of swings and seesaws awaiting exploration further down from the pond and the smiley-faced man.

"This is unbelievable," Max said. He wasn't sure where to go next, an enormous leafy green wall of plants and trees blocked them. "How big is this park, exactly?"

"Fifteen thousand miles," Cruz said.

"That's *not* a park," Ibbie said, looking up at the tall trees. "–It's a jungle. Do people really walk around in there?"

Franz wanted to know if they'd get to use machetes.

Dr. Cruz said the park was the home of the Yanomami. "They call it a park, but it's a rain forest. Thirty-five thousand people live in there," he said, nodding at the periphery of the jungle. They could hear the sounds of birds and the chatter and call of other things. "I'm guessing there are two hundred, maybe two-hundred and fifty villages."

"No machetes for you guys," Max said, big smile at Franz and Ibbie. Neither of them smiled back. Ibbie and his nephew had very worried looks. Max said, "There are people your age and a lot older who've spent their lives in that forest."

"We'll be sharing a village," Cruz said. "The Yanomami are very generous and good hearted people. We can learn from them. I met the leader of our particular village, a woman. Very old. One of the men told me she's over a hundred. Another one said, a hundred and fifty. Of course, nobody really knows, even the woman doesn't know."

"My Auntie's old," Ibbie said. A wistful look, Max thought. As if the girl was already regretting their trip. "Auntie says she's seventy-two, but I think she lies about her age. She's a *lot* older than that. It's funny, you know? Imagine being so old you think seventy-two is young."

Max's attention had shifted away from his nephew's friend. He was feeling better, less anxious. It surprised him, this blooming calmness. Even with all the unknowns beyond the tall dark-leaf wall and the distant squawk of animals, peace curled about him. The calmness didn't last, though. Max had spotted a narrow dirt path to his left, a way into the Parima Tapirapeco. He also saw a shadow of something wriggled across that path, leaving tiny swirls in the dust.

PREPARING FOR THE WOLF

"Come and 'ave a look at this, it's dead, just lying there, stone dead!"

– Metamorphosis

San Francisco de Paula
Outside Havana

WHERE DO YOU start? Kopecky thought; and answered his own question, you start where you left off and see where it takes you. His second thought was more an image – Lottie Hoffmann shooting another two bullets into his good knee. Less than an hour ago the inspector had left Havana Hospital. Doctor Castiel had told Kopecky he needed a few more days.

"You risk an infection," Castiel said, his tone more clinical than personal. Martin Castiel was an orthopedic surgeon. A middle-aged man who looked positively meticulous, his white lab coat pressed and buttoned, his fingernails manicured. He wore rimless glasses and his white hair was combed straight back. He said, "I can't keep you against your will. But I must give you a strong warning. The knee is a delicate thing. Think of what you'd miss if you had no knees, my dear Kopecky. You couldn't run. You couldn't walk in a relaxed manner. And that's just for starters. We're forever taking the knee for granted. We leap. We jump. We sit. Who pays attention to the knee? No one, not a

single soul. It's depressing. We're oblivious to our bodies, especially the much neglected knee. We climb mountains. We leap out of airplanes. We race on treadmills. I find this attitude unfathomable. We're a bunch of anatomical illiterates, no better than the average American. And some Europeans."

Inspector Kopecky was hobbling about the opened closet, dressing himself. He'd already strapped his holstered weapon tight against his wrinkled blue dress shirt. Now he was buckling his gray gabardine suit pants, zipping up the fly. "I'll need a cane," the inspector told him. "Can you do that for me? I don't want to fall all over myself."

"This isn't a good idea," the doctor said.

"You don't know this individual." The inspector slipped on his suit coat. "It's the *only* idea. It's what I have to do. The last time I saw her she was holding a dead woman in her arms, a person she'd known for a good twenty-five years – longer, probably – the only person who'd ever really loved her. Shot her through the front door of their home."

"It happens," the doctor said.

"You mean jealousy?" The inspector didn't wait for a response. "No, this is about letting the outside in, a betrayal of privacy. A betrayal for having someone's back. If you can't trust the person who shares your life and thoughts, who can you trust?"

"You're sympathetic."

"I knew her before she'd killed anyone." Kopecky looked out the hospital window at the cloudless morning, sunlight glittering the mint green walls of his tiny hospital room. "–A beautiful child," he said. "Dark hair, dark eyes. I was enamored. And, yes, sympathetic, too. There was a sweetness about her. I actually thought people who were so lovely and charming had no reason to kill anyone."

"You must've been young," the doctor said.

"Very young, yes. She had a sweetness about her then, not a line on her face. Even her voice had an innocence." Kopecky sat on the edge of his unmade hospital bed, resting his knee for a moment. He thought about meeting Lottie years later. "You can really see a person's life in their face. That was the first time I realized what life does to a person, how it devours sweetness, takes everything charming. And what's left are sharp lines and a darkness about the eyes. What's left are thin, dry lips and the expression you use the most. If you were angry most of the time, that's what a face tells us. Older people can't help but be honest. Our faces become so truthful over time. I didn't realize any of that 'til I saw her again. You see that hardness and you know life hasn't been good."

"Don't do this thing, Inspector."

"Doctor, I've been doing what I do forever." Kopecky stood and stretched, his fingers rubbing the lower arc of his back. He said, "I used to drink a lot – vodka, mostly. Loved fucking vodka, the colder the better. I haven't had a drink now for sixteen years. April, 24th, I put the glass down. I'd always thought evil was matter of circumstance. It didn't matter if it was a gene you didn't ask for, or the way your mama and daddy treated you. By the time I took notice of all the vodka bottles in my trash can, I knew kidding myself wasn't an option."

Dr. Castiel reached into the shadowy back of the closet where Kopecky had retrieved his clothing and brought out a metal and tan plastic cane and handed it to the inspector. "It's adjustable," the doctor said. "Let me see you walk." The inspector obliged. Castiel watched him, nodding. Then the doc said, "Avoid running, you don't want to wake up that knee. It's the sort of pain that'll get you crazy."

"I may have to grin and bear it, doc."

"I'm not certain of much, Inspector. But I tell you what, you run on that knee and you won't be grinning."

Kopecky didn't answer. He'd started thinking about Lottie Hoffmann and the years he'd known her. A teenager daring enough to grab his interest – drunk and beating up on a boy twice her size, stealing a car or two, or wearing five or six unpaid for dresses out of a store. He could almost dismiss these things as what some kids do. What his dear mom, rest her old soul, called "growing pains." But innocence can disappear without notice. Once Kopecky caught Lottie beating her dog, a honey colored cocker spaniel she called Mr. Flip. He'd been driving though her neighborhood and there Lottie was, almost 20 then, leash in one hand, the other hand balled up and socking that dog. Mr. Flip was on his back, paws in the air, squealing. Kopecky had leaped on the girl, his body spread over her like a big paper weight, his right hand cupping the girl's fist. "Get off me, fat boy," she'd said.

Kopecky couldn't believe himself. Sure, he remembered the helpless, whining dog. Who doesn't remember a pleading dog? In all fairness, a dog with the teeth of a wolf who doesn't use those teeth is equally disturbing. And sure, he remembered Lottie's cruelty. She was definitely one cruel bitch. Let's never forget that. But was he really a *fat* boy? And did she mean it, or was she just annoyed at the moment, the way people get? Hit goes through a person's mind.

COMFORTING THE DECEASED

"... he walked by himself between the empty pews, and the size of the cathedral seemed to be just the limit of what a man could bear."

— The Trial

Iglesia de San Francisco de Paula
San Francisco de Paula

AT A TIME somewhere between 1:30 and 2:00 AM, Lottie Hoffmann began digging a grave for Aria Maloof near a cypress tree in the cemetery behind the *Iglesia de San Francisco de Paula*. She'd stolen her neighbor's red and white '55 Chevy Bel Air to tote Aria to the church. By 4:23 AM Aria's body was buried wrapped in a white sheet. Lottie lay next to the fresh mound of soil that covered the new grave. The shovel now rested between her folded arms, Lottie sleepy and curled beside the Chevy.

What possessed you to share our lives with a fuckin' priest? She still couldn't get over Aria's logic, or her *lack* of logic. What was I supposed to do with you? Say, all is forgiven? Say, don't worry? You understood the repercussions. It wasn't like you and I were strangers, you knew my business. You were never an innocent.

Someone was behind her.

Lottie heard the footsteps on the gravel path. Pink

247

traces of daylight had begun to cut the darkness. She dug into the pocket of her denim jacket, retrieving her Beretta, laying the weapon on her lap. Maybe the noise was just her imagination, but a person can't be too careful. Then Lottie thought, fucking Kopecky. That's when she heard a bullet sink into the trunk of the tree just above her head – above her fucking *head*. Immediately, she crawled behind the red and white Bel Air. Everything stayed quiet.

Quiet ...

Quiet ...

Shit. No surprise here. This asshole knew her too well; knew her moves, knew her weak spots. I'm too damned predictable, Lottie thought. Aria used to tell me that, too. Kopecky was a watcher and he had watched her for years. He'd studied how she answered his questions, what got her upset, what calmed her. When Lottie was around him, she could feel herself collapsing back into her younger days – he the grown up cop, she the bad teen who liked stirring up his shit. I should've left Aria at the house, she thought, let her rot. The dead don't care what you do. They expect nothing. The dead never pout or get offended or want you to love them in a way that would betray your whatever, *values*.

Just wait here, Lottie instructing herself. You don't move and you wait. Five minutes, ten minutes, whatever it takes. Kopecky is a talker, he'll show himself. He loves talking, always yak-yak- yak. He makes little speeches. Like he wants to save my ass or fuck me – I never knew with him. Both, probably. Kopecky's weak, the guy should've been a social worker. Lottie peered round the Chevy, beyond the new grave and into the muted dark colors of a new day.

"Where are you? she whispered. "You and your gun, where are you?" Lottie couldn't believe the guy was here again. She'd shot him in the knee. Saw the bullets go in – *twice*, the *same* knee. Sheer luck. You mess up a guy's knee and that's that. He'll be hobbling the rest of his life –Tiny fucking Tim. Kopecky was like the robot in that old movie, the one who keeps coming after you no matter what you do to it. You could chop him up into little pieces and all the little pieces would come after you.

"Lottie." The voice came from the shadows in front of her, the dark blue and pinkish light. *His* voice, definitely, Inspector Friendly, "... hey, how you doing?"

Great, here we go, she thought.

"You really did a number on my leg," Kopecky said. The words hovered out there, no face, no body, just words between the trees and the tombstones. He whispered, "Nice shooting, I should give you that. Better than I could do." The cemetery became silent again. Lottie waited, listening to the sound of Havana Bay a block away, water splashing against rocks. She heard him say, "You do know I won't leave here without you, yes?"

She kept quiet.

"The woman loved you, Lottie."

Mind your fucking business, that was what she wanted to tell him, but she knew this was what he wanted – to start a "dialog." One of his favorite expression – "We need to start a *dialog*," he'd tell her. "How can we reach an understanding, if we can't communicate to one another? And it's not like I'm a stranger. Am I right? You know I'm right. We've got history, Lottie. We go back, don't we? Years. Hell, *decades*." Kopecky loved inching his way into her tender places. Lottie imagined saying stupid shit to him, getting all bothered by his clever words. She could picture the old asshole grinning in the shadows. Got her, he'd say to himself. She's mine, now, boys and girls. Gotcha, bitch. Gotcha by the tits.

"What was her name, again?" Kopecky said, so respectful, so humble-like. "God, it's on the tip of my tongue. 'Aria,' wasn't it? Damn pretty name Lottie. People are always liking to pit this one against that one. I don't believe in doing that. Everybody has a story, a way of seeing things. Aria and you had your own separate stories, that's what I think."

After this, Kopecky got quiet. Five minutes, ten minutes, Lottie wasn't sure, exactly. Had he decided to give her an opportunity? She wanted to ask him something. But what? How about, can I walk away? Why not let this current indiscretion slide? She would've liked him to say, 'Go on, girl, escape – for old times.' Yes, for old times. For all those years ago.

"...Dominik?" Lottie said. Immediately she thought, No, *no*. What have you *done*? She bit the edge of her bottom lip hard enough to bring blood.

"Over here," he said, his voice barely audible.

Lottie turned and Dominik Kopecky shot her once in the neck and once in the face. She didn't have time to say anything, no plea, no wait-a-second, no time to charm him, no time to make a noise.

EPILOGUE

A Yanomami Village
National Park Parima Tapirapeco
Amazonas, Venezuela

FRANZ LIKED THE smell of the Longhouse, something between the straw the villagers used for the sides and floor and the enormous dried leaves used for the roof. Moonlight came into the house from the windows and the door chopped into the walls with machetes. It was late and Ibbie was asleep, her pallet next to his. Franz didn't know the exact time. Everyone had given up their watches and phones before entering the village.

That was close to six months ago.

Time didn't simply slow down. It stood still. Franz felt it, too. It felt as if the four of them had stepped into a different dimension – timeless and without anything familiar to quiet them, to give them peace and a feeling of safety. Everything had changed.

It'd been a change where nothing lured them and nothing stirred the soul. Once rain had flooded their little village and they had spent a couple of days sitting on the roofs of the longhouses. Another time the men in the village had to kill male and female jaguar who'd wandered into their camp looking for dinner.

Franz didn't like the jungle, but he kept his feelings to himself. On the other hand Ibbie wasn't nearly as stoic. She complained about it constantly.

"Who lives without a watch?" She'd say to no one in particular but loud enough for everyone to know her discontent. "— And a *phone*. My God, nobody walks around without a phone. That's crazy. Suppose somebody needs to get in touch?"

"We're in a jungle," Franz would reminder her.

"Life just doesn't *stop*," she'd say.

"It does in a jungle."

Her complaints weren't about just a phone or a watch. The heat and the bugs bothered her, too. Franz reminded her that their symptoms had vanished. His hand was normal, not a web between the fingers, not a darkening of the skin. Ibbie's symptoms had also vanished. Her eyes were clear, her shoulders without a hint of greenish shell. The same could be said of his Uncle Max and Stephan Cruz.

"We have no choice," Dr. Cruz had told everyone. "We must let go of the life that brought us here. Just look at us. I don't know about you, but I've never felt better. No symptoms, my legs are stronger. I can't remember a time when I've felt this good." The man turned to Max. "And see how healthy your nephew and Ibbie are looking, my friend. I bet you're feeling pretty good yourself – go on, admit it."

Max shrugged then gave a quick, throw away smile.

"See, *see*." Stephan ginned back at Max. "Ha! I thought so. Everybody feels great in the jungle. Nothing like it in the world." Dr. Cruz believed in letting go of one's appliances – that's what he called watches, phones, computers and the rest –"appliances" – and he believed this was a *very* big part of the cure. He liked saying how too much information could distort our thinking and overwhelm the person with rage and a craving to subdue the various opposing camps.

Most of Dr. Cruz's talk gave Franz a headache. Now the boy was glancing about the longhouse, all shadows and moonlight. There were eleven villagers living with Franz and his group. All were sleeping, most snoring or making odd sounds in the backs of their throats. Beyond the open door, he could see Max and Dr. Cruz sitting on the ground and talking near the last embers of a campfire. Franz decided to sneak closer to the door to hear what the two men were saying.

"My mother – rest her – used to go to *Divoka Sarka* in the summer," Max was saying to Cruz. "She had terrible back pain. The woman needed to use a cane to get from the living room to kitchen in our tiny house. But every year she and her brother would go to *Divoka Sarka*, a lovely park with many trees and a clear beautiful lake fed by an underground stream. So very beautiful. The lake was plenty cold, too, let me tell you, but Mother loved it." A warm breeze fluttered the last, small flames of their campfire. Max said, "She tossed her cane in less than a week – less than a *week*, can you imagine, Stephan? It wasn't the lake, either. The lake had no special powers, nothing like that. The dear woman just left whatever cares she had in Prague."

"Precisely," Stephan said. "–A wise woman."

"Here's what I believe." Max was absently doodling something in the dry, loose dirt with a stick as he talked. "Healing like beauty is in the heart of the beholder. I'm not talking about a broken leg or the flu. What I'm speaking of is what we think and what we feel and how such things shape our world. Any good priest would tell you the same."

"Yes, this is not much different than my own thought," Cruz agreed. He stood, looking at the campfire, stretching his back. "It's not first time we've left the familiar to lead less destructive lives."

Franz needed to get his uncle alone.

The boy rested his back against the straw wall, his bare feet on the cool straw floor. He needed to tell Max how living in this place wasn't for Ibbie and it wasn't for him.

He didn't like going without a watch. It felt as if his mind was floating in dark, endless space. Having time and deciding what to do with time was more important than he had ever imagined. Franz remembered his father losing his own watch. How the man panicked, his eyes becoming big and crazed. He'd looked everywhere – under his bed, in the crevasses of the living room sofa and his favorite chair. The search had gone on for days until his father finally gave up and raced to the neighborhood jeweler to buy a new one.

"Time is who we are," Karl Hoffmann had once told his son. "It's terrible to admit, Franz. People hate being addicted, believe me. To *any*thing. Yet we're always figuring the years, months, weeks and days of every damn thing. It's true. As long as we know there's an end to us, we'll obsess about it."

Franz didn't know about that. The boy just didn't want to live in the jungle. He'd rather take his chances. Ibbie wanted to take her chances, too. He saw Ibbie getting more upset with each day. The thought and feel of the pain they'd both endured became less and less with time and boredom.

"I'd rather deal with how I am, symptoms and all, and keep my friends," she told him. "Besides, a lot of people are like us. Remember?"

He did remember.

Franz would talk to his uncle tomorrow, or definitely the day after– whenever he felt the time was right. He'd take Max aside, away from Dr. Cruz, and plead with him, if he had to. And should Ibbie not want to help, he'd do it alone. It would be difficult, very difficult. Uncle Max and Dr. Cruz liked the jungle, that was what it looked like to Franz. Maybe they were too old to understand the value of new friends. The boy thought about the young Cuban girls sitting on the seawall at night and listening to music and watching the old shiny cars passing them as if the cars were strutting in a slow, never ending parade. He liked the sound of the bay and how the waves hit against the gray stone wall, the way the water sprayed down on everyone, a quick, cold rain. Being young was so much different than being old. Your life waits for you when you're young. Older people forget that. They don't understand how life can drive you crazy.

Thank you for reading.
Please review this book. Reviews help others find New Pulp Press and inspire us to keep providing these marvelous tales.

If you would like to be put on our email list to receive updates on new releases, contests, and promotions, please go to NewPulpPress.com and sign up.

ABOUT THE AUTHOR

Ron Savage has published numerous novels, a story collection and over a hundred and twenty-five stories worldwide. He has both a BA and MA in psychology and a doctorate in counseling, all from the College of William and Mary. Ron has worked primarily as a therapist. He has also worked as a newspaper editor, actor and broadcaster.

www.ingramcontent.com/pod-product-compliance
Lightning Source LLC
Chambersburg PA
CBHW060537260626
47161CB00003B/942